Nae

Too Real To Be Fake: Welcom
A novel by Naeem M. Kearney

Editor: Rachel Wagner (www.Rachel-Wagner.com)
Graphic Designer: Boris Sarafimov (bokasmoka21@gmail.com)

This is a work of fiction. Names, characters, and incidents either are the product of the author's imagination or are used fictitiously. Any resemblance to real people, living or dead, actual events, organizations, and or establishments are intended to give the fiction a sense of reality and authenticity. Other names, characters, places and incidents are either products of the author's imagination and are used fictitiously.

ISBN-978-0-578-20125-2

Too Real To Be Fake!

WELCOME TO MURDAVILLE

Introduction

Five shots rang off. POW! POW! POW! POW! POW! Every shot seemed louder than the next, and little Jamal stood there terrified that a stray bullet might accidentally hit him. He witnessed the entire incident and saw what caused the shooting, however he wasn't too scared because he knew he wasn't the intended target.

Jamal's dog sprinted away into the dark, shaken up by the loud thunder sound caused by the gunshots. Without thinking, he ran after his dog as if he never heard the shots fired. Amirrah, Jamal's mother, let out a terrifying scream as she watched her son dash into danger. She stood there helplessly and prayed that a stray bullet wouldn't hit her son. Her voice caught his attention in mid sprint, and he froze in his tracks.

Everyone else around Jamal was yelling, ducking, and running into the buildings trying to take cover. Jamal turned around and started running back towards his mother, who was squatting down waving her hands, signaling for him to hurry up. As Jamal was running back, the shooter shot three more times, and Jamal's body flinched every time another shot rang off.

The impact of the bullets sent Darnel's body crashing into the ground, letting him and everyone else know that he was the intended target. Jamal fell into his mother's lap as he watched in disbelief as Darnel's lifeless body laid on the pavement. Jamal always heard gun shots at night and heard about people dying, but never witnessed how still a person's body is moments after death. That day changed Jamal forever.

Jamal grew up around both men and knew them personally. The shooter was Travis. Travis looked exactly how the streets treated him. He looked rough, like the world never gave him a break, but he still had a soft spot in his heart for his daughter, India. India was Jamal's first crush. The minute he laid eyes on her, he knew she was going to be his someday. The victim was Darnel, his best friend, Jason's older brother. Darnel had it hard as well but had love from his family that couldn't be replaced.

All of them lived in Hayes Homes projects in Newark, New Jersey. Hayes Homes was a housing project that housed all different kinds of people. Jamal would always pass by the same strung out crackheads begging for cash as he entered the bleak building after preschool. The building was uninviting and had nothing but a few weeds and tall grass to greet its occupants, but it was home for Jamal. Darnel and Jason lived in building #326, the same building where Jamal lived just two floors up. Travis grew up in the next building over, building #328.

Jamal was sitting in the living room, on an old green couch his mother purchased with vouchers from Salvation Army. The cushions were worn out from the previous owners and Jamal sank into the middle. He sat there thinking about what had just happened and how hurt his best friend, Jason, was going to be once he found out his older brother got killed. He knew Jason looked up to his brother and that finding out about his death would eat him alive.

Jamal's mind wondered as he reminisced on how Jason always looked up to his brother. He remembered the time Darnel caught Jason in his room sporting his jersey that fit Jason like an oversized dress while mimicking gang signs, which Jason knew nothing about at the time. Jamal silently chuckled to himself before his mother walked into the room.

"Why did Travis have to kill Darnel? Why didn't he just fight him?" Jamal asked his mother.

Amirrah knew she couldn't give him a logical answer that he would understand at the age of five so she replied the only way she knew how. "I don't know Mally. I really don't know."

Jamal being so young at the time, all he knew about death was once someone died, they never came back. He looked at his mother with teary eyes and said, "Mommy, I don't want to die."

She hugged him while rubbing his back. "Don't worry son you're going to live to be 100 years old," she softly whispered.

Life would never be the same for Jamal. Witnessing so much violence at such a young age left him traumatized. Seeing Darnel die took a piece of innocence away from Jamal that he would never get back.

Life in the projects was rough for Amirrah and Jamal. Amirrah's top priority was her family, and she tried her best to make sure her son never went to bed hungry. She worked full time at Continental Airlines picking up heavy luggage to keep food on the table and a roof over their heads. She would drop Jamal off at school before she went to work, then he would go to Jason's house after school until his mother came home from work at 5 o'clock.

After Darnel was murdered, there was nothing but chaos in Jason's house. Jason's mother relapsed and started getting high again off crack cocaine. Jason and his little sister, Karen, would always be left home alone. When she was home, she was too busy with different men in and out of the apartment to pay the children any attention. Even though Jason was young himself, he felt the need to protect his sister. Amirrah worked so much she had no idea what was really going on, all she knew was she didn't have the extra money for a babysitter and Jason's mother would watch Jamal basically for free.

Jamal and Jason would always roam the projects unattended while the older guys would be selling drugs or playing dice. The drug addicts would be lurking around the projects in search of a scheme to make money to buy more drugs. In the projects, little boys rode bikes, played tops, flipped on old dirty mattresses, played chase, and threw rocks. While the little girls played with their click clacks, jumped rope, and made up steps. Stolen cars would speed by or drive into the big field to put on a show by pulling up the emergency brake while turning the steering wheel and pressing the gas, causing the car to spin in circles while an audience watched on in awe.

With all that action going on in the projects, all Jamal wanted to do was talk to the drug dealers and get a better understanding of life. They had all the fly clothes, nice jewelry, hot cars, and lots of money. It just didn't make since how his mother worked so hard but had nothing.

By the time Jamal was ten years old, his mother was buying him clothes like Old Navy and Fila's, but he wanted Guess jeans and Air Jordan's like the drug dealers wore. His mother would always complain about bills when he asked her for money, but she never explained to him that she had to pay rent, PSE&G, her car note, insurance, and take care of him, herself, and his two-year-old brother, Amod, without any help. While looking at the game from the outside and watching his mother work long hard hours just to make enough to barely get by, choosing between the two wasn't hard at all. Since he was a kid, Jamal knew he didn't want to live the life of a working person. The image of being a drug dealer was so fascinating, and his mind was made up as a child that that's what he wanted to do.

Five years had passed since he witnessed Darnel's death, and he went from being a curious little kid to a heartless little boy. He learned basically everything he knew from watching the streets and talking to drug dealers. His entire look on life had changed. His mentality was kill or be killed.

Being as though it was only Jamal, Amod, and his mother living alone (with the exception of a few strange men from time to time), Jamal never had anyone he could converse with to fill his void of curiosity. There were times when he attempted to have conversations with his mother, and he would ask so many questions that she would get aggravated to the point that she would tell him to shut the fuck up. As a kid, he didn't understand how his mother felt after working long hours, then having to come home to clean and cook. All she wanted to do was relax and catch up on sleep.

He never liked when his mother was mad and began to just avoid asking her anything. When he began to isolate himself, Amirrah noticed it and would ask him why he was so quiet. Jamal was just confused, but he found a way to fulfill some of the emptiness he was feeling at home while out in the streets. Most of his answers came from a drug dealer named Shice.

Shice was a young up-and-coming drug dealer who lived in his projects. He was well respected and was known for starting trouble. He earned the nickname Shiesty from getting cool with people until he knew enough information to rob them. He was loyal when it came to his friends, but everybody else was a potential come up in his eyes.

One day Jamal asked Shice, “Why don’t you get mad when I ask you a lot of questions? Everybody else do.”

To which Shice replied, “Niggas be on some fake shit! Real niggas understand and respect that the lil homies wanna know shit. The game was given to me by the old heads, so it’s only right that I give it to the youth. These niggas out here on some fake shit but I’m **Too Real to Be Fake!** You feel me, lil man?”

Chapter 1: Out the Projects

It was June of 1999. Jamal now was sixteen. He and his family moved out of the projects and were now residing in a subsidized unit on High Street in Newark. Jamal's little brother, Amod was eight and only lived in the projects for a short part of his life. He was too young at the time to understand as much as Jamal did. To Jamal, the new townhouse felt like a baby mansion. They finally had a front and back door, a porch, and stairs in their house instead of the piss odor staircases in the projects. They also had a backyard with a sand box and swing, two bathrooms, their own rooms, and cable television. All the saving Amirrah did finally paid off, and Jamal loved every bit of it.

*****

"What's good, Mally G?" Snub yelled to Jamal from a distance while walking towards him with his hand in the air.

Snub was one of the first people Jamal became cool with in his new neighborhood. Snub witnessed Jamal get into a conflict with kids from Prince Street Projects at school and even though he was outnumbered, he didn't show any signs of fear and didn't back down. Snub admired his heart, so he came to Jamal's aid and made sure he didn't get jumped. They had been close friends ever since. Besides his best friend Jay, whom he barely saw anymore due to the distance of their houses, Snub was Jamal's closest friend.

"What's good with you, my nigga?" Mally G replied before embracing his friend Snub with a handshake.

"Shit, I just came from this lil bitch house on Spruce Street. Would you believe that hoe got the nerve to say I gave her a STD?"

"Word!" Mally G said in between laughs while pointing at Snub. "I told you about fucking all them dirty ass bitches raw. You probably don't even know who gave you that shit."

"Yes I do. It was Meeka, Keeda, or Brandy. Shit, it was probably her ass and she try'na blame me." Snub paused, then looked up in the air while in deep thought before saying, "Oh yeah, it could of been Keena dirty ass too." They both broke out into laughter as they walked into Mally G's house.

"Mally G, what's good? You try'na go to the skating rink tonight?" Snub asked.

"Hell yeah! Shit from nine to one, right?"

"Yeah and it's gone be hella hoes in there," Snub said while opening the refrigerator as if he was in his own house. He pulled out a pot and made himself a bowl of leftover spaghetti.

Amirrah entered through the back door when Snub was almost done and frowned when she saw him eating. "Jamal, no company!" she yelled as she dropped her purse and keys on the kitchen counter.

Snub jumped up without excusing himself and left out through the back door leaving his plate on the table. The minute the spring door slammed shut, she started drilling Mally G.

"Jamal, what in the hell did I tell you about bringing your lil dirty ass friends in here and letting them eat up all the damn food? Now when it ain't no food in here don't come crying talking about you hungry! Where in the hell is your brother?" she screamed.

"I think he's still upstairs sleep," Mally G answered with a low tone knowing his mother was mad at him.

"Wash them damn dishes!" Amirrah said before storming up the stairs.

Mally G was in deep thought as he began to wash the dishes. *I'm tired of this shit! I gotta get the fuck out of here. Now she probably be on some bullshit and don't let me go skating. Fuck that! I'm going. I ain't beat.*

Ring, ring, ring! The sound of the house phone snapped him out of his trance.

"Jamal, get the phone!" Amirrah yelled from upstairs as Mally G was already heading towards it.

"Hello."

"Can I speak to Mally G?"

"Who this?"

"Jason."

"Jay, what's good, bruh!" Mally G said excitingly, happy to hear from his best friend.

"Chilling, man. I gotta get the fuck out this house though, my mother tripping."

"Shit, my mother tripping too," Mally G said.

"Nah, I'm talking bout I think my mother started fucking with that shit again. She in this bitch cleaning shit that's already clean and looking for change in the couches."

"Damn, Jay. Where ya lil sister at?"

"Karen at my grandmother's house."

"Aight, well look I'ma see if my mother will let you spend the night over here."

"Aight, go see right now and let me know what's good."

"Aight, just give me a few minutes cause she fake mad. I'ma hit you right back."

After cleaning up, Mally G hesitated before walking up the stairs because he knew his mother was still mad at him.

"Mommy," he said in a soft tone while standing in her doorway.

"What, boy?"

"I just got off the phone with Jay. He said his mother bugging off drugs. Karen at their grandmother's house, so can he spend the night? I'm finished with the dishes, and I cleaned the stove too."

"How he supposed to get here? I'm tired, I've been working all day, and I'm not about to drive all the way down to Hyatt Court to get him."

"So if he get a ride, can he stay the night?"

"Yeah, and the minute ya'll get loud I'ma take his ass back home."

"Aight. Thanks, mom!" he said joyfully before heading back downstairs.

*****

Later on that day:

Ding dong...

"Jamal, answer the door!" Amirrah yelled across the hall from her room. Mally G lifted up his window and stuck his head out to see who was ringing the doorbell. A huge smile appeared on his face when he saw his best friend.

"Jay, hold on I'm coming down."

He ran down the stairs as fast as he could and opened the door. They embraced each other with a quick handshake and hug.

"Damn, Jay, how you get here?" Mally G asked with a confused look.

Jay put on a devilish smile then pointed to a gray 1992 Acura Legend parked in the parking lot with cheap purple tinted windows. He pulled a flat head screwdriver with a red base out of his pocket and wiggled it in his hand.

Mally G smiled and then lightly pushed Jay's shoulder before saying, "You ain't got the wheel!"

"Nigga, you bugging. You know I'll trunk you to a house," Jay replied. They both started laughing before Mally G quickly changed the subject.

"Yo, we in the rink tonight!" he said excitedly.

"Who all suppose to be going?" Jay asked.

"I know Snub wanted to go. I'm saying now that we g-riding, it's up to us. Matter of fact, lets walk around the corner and see if Snub and them out there."

"Fuck walking. We riding, baby," Jay said while walking out the house with a huge smile.

When they pulled up to the corner of High and Spruce Street, where Snub, BG, Will, and Lil Mar Mar were all hanging out, they all surrounded the vehicle immediately.

Snub approached the passenger side and asked, "Who g-ride is this?"

"Mine!" Jay replied while showing him the screwdriver.

"This block too hot to be sitting here talking, niggas try'na go to the rink or what?" Mally G said impatiently.

Everybody immediately entered the vehicle except Snub.

"Snub, I thought you wanted to go. You coming or what?" Mally G asked as Jay put the car into gear ready to leave him.

"Hold up, Jay!" Mally G snapped because he didn't want to leave Snub.

"I'm saying I wanna go, but I don't trust that lil nigga wheel. Let me drive," Snub replied.

Everyone in the car agreed, "Yeah, yeah. Let Snub drive."

"This my car, ya'll motherfuckers can get out and walk as far as I care," Jay hollered.

Snub crossed his arms and didn't budge. Moments later, two doors opened and BG, Will, and Mar Mar exited the vehicle on cue.

"Come on, Jay. Just let Snub drive this one time," Mally G pleaded, wanting his friends to come.

"I'ma let him drive only on the strength of you, but I'm driving back. If niggas don't trust my wheel they can walk back, fuck that!"

"Snub, come on!" Mally G yelled before Jay got out and got in the back seat.

"I'm letting you know now I'm driving back from the rink!" Jay said aggressively, feeling like he just got punked by letting Snub drive. Snub ignored him and pulled off quickly causing the tires to burn out leaving tire tracks on the concrete.

When they pulled up to Branch Brook Park Skating Rink, the line was all the way around the corner. Snub drove around the parking lot numerous times, yelling out names, trying to get the crowd's attention to show off the car as if he owned it.

"Damn! Park the car so we can get in line! And I'm driving back so give me my screwdriver!" Jay yelled, getting aggravated.

As they approached the line, Snub was greeted by some guys he knew from around the way, and they let everyone squeeze in line with them. Everybody behind them looked on in disgust from seeing them ditch the long line. When they got to the cashier window everybody pulled out money and paid to get in except Will.

"Yo, I ain't got no money."

"Why you gon' wait all the way until we get in here to say you ain't got no money. Ya fat ass better give me my money back too!" Snub said before he paid Will's way in.

When they entered the rink, the music was blasting as Master P's "Bout it Bout it" came through the speakers. *"If you bout it, then say you bout it bout it, bounce bounce bounce fool, if you bout it bout it..."*

The rink was dim lit and packed as they entered in through the double doors. They walked straight to the back, passing the spot to rent skates, heading straight towards where the arcade games were located.

"Let's make a bet," Mally G said smiling while observing all the girls in the crowd. "I bet y'all I could get more numbers than y'all."

"I got five dollars you can't bag more bitches than me!" Snub said before pulling a crisp five-dollar bill out of his pocket.

"I'll bet but we gone take turns starting with you, Snub. We pick the chick, and you bag her. Cause I ain't bout to lose my money cause you bagged a whole lot of ugly bitches," BG said before laughing, knowing Snub had bad taste. Everybody agreed to play the game and left the arcade to start walking around the rink.

Snub was eighteen but looked much older. He was real black with big dark lips and a baldhead. He was 5'11 in height, medium build, and dressed like he had lots of cash. He had an amazing mouthpiece when it came to talking to girls. He was one of those ugly guys you'd see with a pretty girl that made you wonder, "how did an ugly guy like that get her?"

Mally G was sixteen, 5'7 in height, and weighed about 135 pounds. He was skinny but always wore oversized clothes. He had a brown skin complexion and considered himself handsome. He had little box braids that he always kept neat. There was something still innocent about him, despite growing up in the streets. Mally G was a little shy but had a lot of confidence in himself and had a slick mouth once he opened up.

BG was sixteen but looked much older. He was brown skinned with a lot of facial hair, giving him that grown man look. He was the same height as Mally G but weighed slightly more than him. He had a lot of older women, which made girls his age a piece of cake when it came to bagging them.

Jay was also sixteen. He and BG were around the same height and weight. He was light skinned and damn near looked Puerto Rican. He had no facial hair, with the exception of a shadow of a mustache and a few strings on his chin, making him look even younger. He had 360 waves spinning on his head and was handsome enough to be a model. Jay was what you'd consider a pretty boy. He wore more fitted clothes than the rest and always matched his shirt with his kicks. He was a professional when it came to girls and all the young girls loved him.

Will was fifteen, fat, and sloppy with a little nappy afro. He didn't take care of himself. He was always ashy and had chapped lips. He didn't have too many girls in his life, which made him try to wife every girl that gave him a chance. He knew his game was in the basement and avoided pushing up on girls.

Lil Mar Mar was fourteen but looked even younger. He had long braids and a little innocent face. He was Snub's little brother but looked nothing like him. Snub made sure Lil Mar Mar stayed fly and kept money in his pockets. He knew all the young girls liked him but was too shy to make a move.

After making their way to the skate rink, everybody took their skates off and the rink became a dance floor. They had been playing their game to get numbers for about an hour. Jay was already in the lead with seven numbers. It was Snub's turn and then Jay was next up again after him.

"Bag her!" Mar Mar said to his big brother while pointing to a cute red bone chick standing alone. She had light brown curly waves and nice pink full lips. Snub approached her with a smile on his face.

"How you doing, sexy? What's your name?"

"Candy," she replied.

"What you got that name cause you sweet or because you taste as good as you look?" Snub said before licking his lips.

"Boy, you crazy," she replied.

"You right, I'm crazy over you and its crazy how good you look. Real talk, ma, I don't even be doing this because I'm a little shy, but when I saw you I couldn't help but try my luck and I hope I'm lucky. Please tell me I'm lucky," Snub said while putting his hands together as if he were praying.

Once she started smiling, he knew he had her. After about three minutes into the conversation, he was walking back towards them waving a piece of paper.

"That's six numbers! It's on you Jay, and I'm picking her because they keep picking these easy bitches."

As they walked through the crowd Snub yelled out, "Bag her!" while pointing to a pretty, thick Puerto Rican girl with long straight hair walking with a Spanish guy holding hands.

"Get the fuck outta here. She with a nigga already!" Jay said aggressively.

"You talk all that pimp pretty boy shit. Let me see where ya game really at. She counts for five numbers if you bag her," Snub said, trying to hype him up.

Jay must have caught the battery because he walked off yelling "I'm going for twelve!" while heading straight towards the couple by the back of the rink.

"Ma, can I talk to you for a couple of seconds?" Jay asked while staring the girl square in the eyes. He caught her off guard, but his cockiness and sex appeal made her blush unconsciously. The Spanish guy with her was puzzled. He thought maybe his girl had known the guy, but once he realized what was going on, he became furious.

"Yo, dawg, that's my girl you talking to!" the guy muttered as his face became beet red.

Jay ignored him and continued his conversation as if the guy wasn't even there. The instant she started laughing, her boyfriend couldn't keep in his frustration. He swung a sloppy right hook that landed directly on Jay's chin, causing him to stubble back before he caught his footing. Before he could recover, two more wild punches landed on his nose and forehead.

Mally G noticed the scuffle and tried to run over to help, but Snub held him back and said, "Hold on, see if he can hold his own first."

Jay was trying his hardest to gain control over the fight, but the Spanish guy was just too big and strong over him. After multiple blows to the face, Jay finally fell down onto one knee and before he knew it, the guy's boot was flying towards his face. With no other options, Jay reached into his pocket and pulled out his screwdriver. In one motion, he pushed up off the floor and rushed towards the Spanish guy. Jay stabbed him numerous times in the stomach causing him to fall to the floor in a fetal position. He was crouched over lying on the floor holding his stomach as Jay continued to stab him three more times in the back finishing him before running towards the exit. When the lights came on, everybody frantically ran towards the exit after seeing the guy lying in a pool of blood.

All of them made it to the car around the same time and knew the police would definitely be arriving any minute.

"Let me drive just in case we get into a chase!" Snub asked as they approached the vehicle.

"Motherfucker, you could walk!" Jay snapped before entering the car. He pulled out the bloody screwdriver and sparked the engine to life. With no other choice, everyone entered the car. Jay pulled off fast without turning on the headlights as he heard the police sirens from a distance.

"Cut the fucking lights on!" Snub barked from the back seat. Jay did as he was told and continued to drive, missing the exit.

"Yo! Yo!" everyone screamed.

Jay pressed on the brakes, bringing the car to a halt before putting it in reverse. As he was backing up, a cop car approached from behind and flashed their lights on them signaling to pull over. Jay's heart immediately dropped when he saw the lights in the rearview mirror, and he pulled off as quickly as he could as the tires screeched. The siren on top of the police vehicle came alive as they proceeded to chase after the fleeing vehicle.

"This is patrol car 973. We're in pursuit of a gray four door Acura Legend, possible stolen and allegedly involved in a 187. We're heading south bound down the 200 block of Norfolk Street, please send back up immediately."

Luckily for Jay there wasn't too much traffic. He drove down Norfolk Street, which turned into Irvine Turner Boulevard doing about 70 miles per hour.

Once he got into a more familiar area, Snub yelled out, "Go to the hood so we can jump out!"

Another cop car appeared in front of them as if it came out of nowhere. By this time, there were so many cop cars behind them it looked like a carnival full of lights when Jay looked into the rearview mirror. After seeing the stampede of cop cars behind them, he turned up 18th Avenue knowing he had to hit some corners to lose his tail.

Snub screamed out, "What the fuck you doing? Why you ain't go towards the hood? Make a right turn, right there!"

Jay made a right, almost hitting a parked car by inches.

"Make another right!" Snub yelled.

Jay tried to turn, but the car was going too fast and broke down too late. Jay lost control of the car and they crashed head on into a light pole. The impact of the car hitting the light pole caused the airbags to burst hitting Jay and Mally G in the face. Both boys were dazed for a split second until they came into realization.

They jumped out and continued fleeing on foot. The police surrounded the area in an attempt to capture their suspects. Mally G and Jay ran down a narrow alley as a skinny Hispanic officer ran after them. A police vehicle cut directly in front of them as they entered the street, and they appeared to be trapped. Mally G jumped over the hood of the car, and Jay ran around the front. It seemed impossible to get away as cops swarmed in from all directions. Mally G jumped a fence leading into a backyard while Jay trailed right behind him. A purebred red nose pitbull came running out of a doghouse and its mouth just missed Jay's foot by inches as he hurdled over another fence. The sight of the huge dog made the cop stop dead in his tracks, allowing them to get a nice stretch on the officers.

After running for what seemed like an hour and jumped what seemed like one hundred gates, they realized they had lost their tail. They began to walk at a rapid pace, attempting to catch their breath.

"Yo, you think Snub and them got away?" Mally G asked in between breaths as he recalled everything that just occurred.

"I don't know. I think I saw them grab Lil Mar Mar, though. Shit got real hectic. I hope they got away."

Moments later they made it back to High Street and saw BG and Will sitting in front of an old Catholic church. They both jumped up in excitement when they saw Mally G and Jay.

"How the fuck did ya fat ass get away?" Mally G asked after he walked up and embraced them with a handshake.

"My cousin, Menace, saw us running and gave us a ride. I thought we was about to get bagged," BG answered before Will could utter a word.

"Do you think Snub and his lil brother got caught?" Will asked out of concern.

"I don't know. Jay said he seen them grab Mar Mar, so nine times out of ten they got Snub too, I hope…"

"Oh shit!" BG said cutting Mally G off.

"There go Snub right there!" He pointed to a person walking up the hill from a distance.

Will squinted his eyes before nodding his head and agreeing. "That is Snub!"

When Snub finally approached them his clothes were drenched and a foul odor escaped from his body.

"Damn! What the fuck is that smell?" Mally G asked while pulling the collar of his shirt over his nose.

"Man, I was hiding in a dumpster for like an hour. I had to damn near swim to the bottom so they wouldn't see me. But fuck all that! Jay, I told ya no wheel having ass to let me drive. Now my lil brother locked da fuck up fucking wit ya bitch ass!" he said approaching Jay with his fist clenched.

"If you wasn't all up in my ear, I wouldn't have crashed!" Jay snarled back while clenching his fist as well.

Mally G jumped in between them before the situation escalated.

"Mally G, fuck that nigga. He ain't from the hood!" BG barked while walking towards them.

Mally G realized a brawl was about to happen and pulled Jay behind him. "Jay, go in the house!" he yelled out while standing in front of Snub and BG so they couldn't get to Jay.

Jay peeped that they were trying to jump him and didn't want to put his best friend in a messed up predicament knowing he had to live around there, so he complied and went into the house. He felt as though they had one up on him and this he would not forget.

Chapter 2: Affiliations

One year later (2000):

After Hayes Home Projects was knocked down, all the drug dealers migrated to different areas. Shiesty A.K.A Shice met a girl on Spruce Street and moved in with her. Little by little he started getting cool with the guys from out there until he made it his home. It had been almost ten years since he had been hanging on High and Spruce Street, and now he was plotting to take it over for good.

"Shice, what's poppin, big bruh!" Snub said before shaking Shice's hand with his pinky and pointer finger out, forming a five-point star.

"I'm bick backin. Try'na paint the city red. Have you seen Mally G lil ass?" Shice responded.

"Nah, why what's good?" Snub asked looking confused.

"I'ma bring him home. I been wanted to turn him Blood. I saw something in him ever since he was a lil nigga running around in the projects. I'ma leave it up to you to bring all the young gangsta's home. I got the older niggas. In a minute, if you ain't Blood, niggas ain't gonna be able to hustle out here. We family, so if you ain't eating off our plate, you ain't eating!"

"Trillz, I feel you, big bruh," Snub replied.

"Just make sure you holla at Mally G for me," Shice stated.

"I got you, big bruh," Snub replied before peacing Shice and walking off. Snub went into his pocket, pulled out his cell phone, and scrolled through his contacts until he found Mally G's number.

Ring, ring, ring…

"Snub, what's good, bruh?" Mally G said after answering his phone.

"I'm bick backin, where you at?"

"At this bitch house down on Astor Street. Why wassup?"

"I need to talk to you about something real important."

"Aight, where you at?

"Just meet me in the townhouses on Quitman Street in five minutes."

"Say no more," Mally G said before he hung up the phone and began walking up the street in deep thoughts. *What the fuck could Snub want to talk about that's so important. I hope he ain't get himself in no bullshit! Where the fuck this nigga at?*

"Mal!" Snub stood up from behind a car waving Mally G over with his hands.

"Snub what's good? What you gotta holla at me about?" Mally G asked curiously.

"Let's go sit over there," Snub replied while pointing to a wooden bench in a grassy area across the street. "Yo, I was just talking to Shice, and he said he want you."

Mally G frowned, "What you mean by 'want me?'"

"He want me to turn you Blood."

Mally G quickly replied, "I fucks with Shice heavy. Shit, I use to look up to him in the projects, but I ain't with that gang shit. Niggas gone respect me for me, not no damn gang. I don't take nothing away from what y'all do, but that shit ain't for me. I'm about green. No disrespect, but that red verses blue shit is stupid, if you ask me."

"Mally G, it ain't what you think. Shit ain't about no fucking red and blue!" Snub said feeling a little bit offended by what Mally just said. "Mal, real talk. We a family and Shice try'na make the family stronger and eliminate the weak. We a street family, and you know we all fuck with you heavy and certain niggas gotta go! How we look at it is it's either niggas with us or you against us!" Snub said with the most serious face Mally G have ever seen.

Mally G just shook his head from side to side before saying, "I don't know what to tell you then."

A red 1997 Honda Civic pulled into the townhouses as they continued to talk. Will and an unfamiliar looking guy exited the vehicle with a certain air about them, wearing red bandannas on their heads.

★★★★★

Across town:

"Where you pushing to, Cuz?" one of Jay's homies asked as he walked towards his car.

"I'm bout to shoot up the hill and scream at Mally G real fast."

"You better stay on ya stacey's going up there around all them slobs."

"I'm good, Cuz, you know I stay on point!" Jay said as he lifted his shirt revealing a chrome P89 Ruger.

"Cuz, you sure you can trust Mally G? He fuck around and be slob himself."

"Watch ya mouth, loc! Mally G my brother, if anything he rolling with us, not against us."

"Aight, Cuz, just cee safe."

Jay drove off heading towards Mally G house. When he got close, he picked up his phone and called him.

"Jay, what's good, bruh?" Mally G said after he excused Snub and then answered his phone.

"Where you at?" Jay asked.

"I'm in the townhouses on Quitman, why what's good? Jay… Jay… Hello?"

Before Mally G could finish his next sentence, Jay's car was pulling into the townhouses. He pulled into a tight spot parked next to the CRX.

When Jay got out of his vehicle, Snub, Will, and Str8 Lace all stared as if they had just seen a ghost. Jay was wearing a navy-blue t-shirt, light blue shorts, and navy-blue Converse Chuck Taylors with thick purple laces. Jay knew all the attention was on him and put on a Kool-Aid smile as he walked up and gave Mally G a quick handshake and hug.

Mally G felt the negative vibe and said, "Bruh, let me holla at you," while walking back towards Jay's car.

"Y'all be having brabs in y'all hood?" Str8 Lace asked aggressively and loud enough for everyone to hear.

Jay kept smiling as he walked towards Mally G.

"Jay, you brab now?" Snub asked while giving him a cold stare.

"Nah, I ain't brab," Jay said in between laughs.

"Then why you got all that flue shit on then?" Snub barked back getting furious at the sight of Jay still laughing.

"Cause I'm Crip, bitch!" Jay snapped as the smile erased from his face and he drew his chrome P89 Ruger from his waistline and pointed it towards Snub's face.

"Jay, fall back!" Mally G yelled while stepping in front of Snub.

A smile appeared back on Jay's face as he lowered his gun and got into his car. Jay knew he made a stance and, in that moment, felt powerful.

"Mally G, I'ma scream at you, bruh," Jay said. Then he turned back to Snub and said, "I'll see you in traffic, Cuz." Then he pulled off.

"Ay, Will, bum here, Blood!" Str8 Lace yelled before he got into his car. Will walked over to his CRX and got into the passenger seat while Snub and Mally G stood there arguing about what had just took place.

"Yo, Mally G, you can't have that brab nigga coming in our hood. We can't go in their hood, plus they our enemies."

"First of all, I could go in any hood I want and that's my best friend. That's the reason I ain't with that dumb gang shit."

"Well this a Blood hood and the next time he come through here he's getting his food ate. So, if you care about that nigga, let him know he ain't welcome around here."

"Man, that's my best friend and I ain't with—" Mally G was interrupted by the sound of a gun cocking back. He found himself looking down the barrel of a gold-plated 44 automatic. "What the fuck you doing?" Mally G yelled harshly with a blank expression on his face.

"Just give me all ya money."

"Word! You gone really rob me?" Mally G asked, not believing what was taking place.

"I don't want to do this to you. Just give me ya money and make it easy on both of us."

Mally G threw his money on the ground and walked away. He felt numb and all kinds of emotions ran through his body. What just took place would take a long time before it registered in his mind and became real. A close friend had betrayed him. At this point, he had no one he could trust except his best friend, Jay. The numb feeling quickly subsided and turned into rage. The only thing on his mind now was revenge.

★★★★★

Meanwhile, across town:

As Jay pulled into the parking lot of Hyatt Court, he noticed his little sister, Karen, sitting in a burgundy Ford Mustang with chrome rims with a guy who looked old enough to be their father. Jay was only one year older than Karen but was always overprotective, being as though he was the only male figure in her life.

Karen was fifteen but was built like she was every bit of twenty-five. She was light skinned with that same Puerto Rican look Jay had. She had long natural silky hair that reached down to the middle of her back and bounced as she walked. Karen already had fully developed breasts that sat up perfect and an ass that could catch any man's attention. Karen learned from an early age what being attractive could get her, despite Jay looking out for her.

Jay's blood rushed to his head at the sight of his little sister being taken advantage of. His eyes were blood shot red as he slammed his car door and walked towards the Mustang. He extracted his gun from his waist and busted out the window using the butt of the gun. The unexpected interruption caused the guy to jump out of his skin.

Before he could even realize what was going on, Jay was pulling him out of the car through the freshly broken window, busting his face the same way he broke the glass. Jay pounded his face repeatedly with the butt of the gun. Smack! Smack! Smack! Smack! Blood was splashing from everywhere.

Karen attempted to grab Jay from behind trying to stop him. "Jay, stop! Please… please… stop!" Karen yelled hysterically in between sobs.

When he finally stopped, the guy was unconscious and lying in a puddle of blood. "What the fuck you doing with this grown ass man?" Jay snapped while turning his focus on his little sister.

Karen was crying so hard that Jay couldn't figure out a word she was trying to say.

"Stop fucking crying and answer my fucking question before I kill this motherfucker!" Jay barked while pointing the gun at the guy's head. The fact that she was crying over the guy only made Jay madder.

"I was just try'na tell you that's Unique's father! He was just dropping me off!" She bawled as tears ran down her face.

Jay felt stupid after he realized what he had just done. Unique was Karen's best friend. Karen had spent the night over Unique's house, and her father was just dropping her off home.

"Damn, Karen, my fault," he said with a puzzled look on his face, not knowing what else to say. Karen just stood there crying. "Karen, come on. We have to get outta here," Jay said while walking towards his car.

"What about Unique's father?"

"By the time he wakes up, he won't remember shit. If anybody ask, he dropped you off and you went upstairs. You ain't see shit and you don't know shit. Now go in the house. I'll be up there in a minute," Jay said as he got into his car.

His phone began to ring as soon as he started the ignition. He looked down and saw it was Mally G.

“Mally G, what’s good, bruh? Hold on, Mally G, slow down, you said what… Word! That nigga robbed you… I thought that was ya man… I told you don’t trust them niggas! Aight, I’ma be at your house in a minute. Aight, one.”

Chapter 3: Who Can I Trust?

Mally G was laying in his bed in deep thought. *I'ma kill this nigga when I catch him. Niggas letting that gang shit get to their heads. I don't believe this shit. That nigga know he ain't built like that.*

His thoughts were cut short by the sound of the doorbell and his phone ringing simultaneously. He knew it was Jay and ran downstairs to open the door. Soon as he opened the door, he noticed blood all over Jay's shirt.

"Jay, what happened?"

"I did some straight bullshit," Jay said in between laughs. He opened up the screen door and walked in, threw his stuff on the glass kitchen table, and took a seat before breaking down the entire story as if he had a whole audience.

"Damn, that's crazy!" Mally G said while shaking his head back and forth appalled by what he had just heard.

"Anyway, what's good with that bitch ass nigga that robbed you? What you try'na do about it?" Jay exclaimed.

"Man, you already know he gotta go!" Mally G replied with a devious look on his face.

"Say no more," Jay said before he pulled out two twin P89 Ruger's and handed one to Mally G.

"I know where that nigga live at too!" Mally G said excitingly before he hurled to his feet.

"Is them real guns ya'll got?" Amod, Mally G's little brother, asked excitedly as he walked into the kitchen still wearing his pajamas.

"No, they BB guns," Mally G responded as he tucked the gun as fast as he could. Jay followed suit.

"Jason, did you kill somebody with that BB gun, why all that blood on ya shirt?" Amod asked as if his innocence slowly dissipated.

"No, Amod, he shot a bird! Now take ya lil bad ass back up stairs and stop asking so many questions," Mally G uttered as he thought back on all the questions he used to ask as a kid.

"Can you teach me how to shoot one day?"

"Yeah, Amod. Now go upstairs!" Mally G said a little aggressive to show Amod he wasn't playing.

After Amod walked off Jay said, "Now where you said that nigga live at?"

"Right around the corner in Brick Towers."

Brick Towers was two tall brick buildings located on High Street a few feet up from Spruce Street. Mostly everybody from High and Spruce Street was cool with the guys from Brick Towers because they all went to the same elementary school and grew up with each other.

"Aight, we gone walk cause I don't want nobody to see my car. Let's get out of here before ya bad ass brother come back downstairs."

"Aight!" Mally G agreed.

It was around midnight and the streets were vacant with the exception of a few cars riding by, drug addicts walking around, and dim streetlights flickering on and off.

"Mally G, you think you ready for this?" Jay asked while looking Mally G directly in his eyes as they were walking.

"Nigga, I was born ready!" Mally G said confidently while looking Jay straight back in the eyes. Mally G's confidence rose from the anger he was still feeling from what had gone down, and no one was going to change his mind about getting revenge.

"When we done, you gotta wear a blue or purple flag for sixty days, aight?" Jay said.

A frown appeared on Mally G's face after hearing that statement. "What the fuck I'm doing that for? I ain't joining no gang, if that's what you think."

"Mally G, you already know we've been best friends since we were born. I love you like my real brother. I wouldn't steer you in the wrong direction. This Crip shit is my family now. You know I lost my brother to the streets and my mother getting high. I've never met my father, my grandmother just died, and the rest of my family doesn't exist in my eyes. Besides you and Karen, my Crip family is all I got."

"Jay, if I turn Crip or not, you'll always be family. Plus, I live on High Street around all Bloods. What I look like turning Crip?"

"Man, fuck them slobs! You ain't gotta live here. You could come down the net with me. If you hang around fake niggas long enough, that fake shit going to rub off on you. Or they going to cross you again. The same niggas you called ya friends robbed you. What type of shit is that! This Crip life is about loyalty. We more like a family than a gang."

"Jay, real talk, the last thing I'm worried about is them niggas crossing me. I'm **Too Real to Be Fake**, so their fakeness rubbing off on me is out too! I'm just not limiting my life. I want to be able to go in Crip and Blood hoods whenever I want without having to worry about no dumb shit. How I look at it, anybody could get it! Motherfuckers gone respect me for me, not no red or blue flag. If a Blood cross you, I'ma bust his ass! If a Crip cross you, I'ma bust his ass! If I fuck with you, I fuck with you, that's just how I am. If you a real nigga, I can fuck with you. If not, then stay the fuck from around me! If it was a gang that dealt with realness, I'll consider it. But that Blood versus Crip shit don't sit right with me."

Jay smiled, "Mally G, that's why I love you. We need more real niggas like you in this world."

They both broke out into laughter as they walked up concrete steps leading to Will's building. Once they got to his door Mally G knocked while Jay waited on the side. Moments later the door opened up, and Will's mother came out with a silk cap wrapped around her head and a young baby in her arms.

"Is Will home?" Mally G asked as if everything was normal.

"No, baby, he didn't come home yet," Will's mother answered in a soft voice.

"Do you know if he staying the night out or not?"

"No, baby. Why is everything alright? Do you need me to give him a message for you?" she asked sounding a bit worried.

"Yeah, tell him—" Mally G was looking for the right words to say before Jay cut him off.

"Yeah, tell him death looking for him," Jay declared with no signs of emotions.

Will's mother had a startled look on her face as the two boys walked away.

When they left from in front of Will's door they staked out in the staircase, patiently waiting for him to come home. After about five hours of waiting, they realized that their stake out was a dud and decided to leave. Jay took Mally G to get a casket of weed from Little Bricks, dropped him off, and headed home leaving one of his P89's behind.

As soon as Jay pulled off, Mally G realized that he didn't have a Dutch Master to roll his weed in. *Damn, I don't feel like walking to the store,* he thought as he began to walk.

As he was walking, he heard a familiar voice call out his name from behind. His heart skipped a beat as he realized whom the voice belonged to. He turned around and saw Will coming out of the building jogging towards him. As Will got closer, without hesitation, Mally G reached into his pocket and pulled out the P89 and aimed directly at Will's forehead before squeezing the trigger. POW! The dynamic force caused his hand to jerk back making the bullet miss Will's head by inches. Will fell to the ground as if he got hit, terrified as he started pleading his case.

"Mally G, please don't kill me! Let me explain what happened!"

"What the fuck could you possibly explain? You robbed me, you bitch ass nigga!" Mally G spat as he put the tip of the gun to Will's forehead as if nothing else in the world mattered.

"Mally G, you know I would have never robbed you, but Str8 Lace made me! He got real high status, and he told me to rob you or else I was food. He said he felt some type of way because you brought a brab in our hood and let him pull out a gun on us. I told him you didn't mean for that to happen, but he wouldn't listen. Then when you and Snub started arguing he said you don't respect

Blood so it's either I rob you or I'm food. If I become food, they will kill me. I went to your house a couple of times last night to give you your money back, but you weren't home. I've been up all night stressing over that shit. I feel like shit. I feel like I betrayed you. I'm sorry, bruh! You know I would never cross you!"

Tears fell down his face as he extended his arm out trying to hand Mally G a knot of crinkled up money. "It's all there," Will said after Mally G lowered the gun and took the money.

"Will, I almost killed you over some bullshit. Str8 Face or whatever the fuck his name is gotta go! We basically grew up together. How you gon' let a nigga you barely know get in between us. Nigga, we've been friends since we were kids—that gang shit fucking shit up!" Mally G exclaimed as his heart was still racing.

Will just sat there in silence as Mally G's words touched a soft spot.

*****

The next day:

Exhausted from the day before, Mally G slept most of the day away. It was 4:00pm, and he was still lying in the bed.

"Wake up, you lil bitch ass nigga!" was all he heard before he opened his eyes to a pistol pointing directly at his face.

*****

At Snub's house:

Boom, boom, boom, boom, Boom, boom!

"Damn! Why the fuck you banging on my door like that? I thought you was the fucking police!" Snub said after he opened the door and saw Will standing there shaking. "What the fuck happened? Why you shaking?"

"Me and BG was standing by the chicken shack and some dude with a mask on tried to rob us. BG had that 44 on him so he tried to reach for it, then the dude shot him up."

"What! Is he good?" Snub asked with a curious look on his face.

Will's voice was trembling, "I don't know. He was alive when the ambulance came, but he got hit like seven times, in the stomach and everything."

"Where the fuck was you at when he was getting shot?"

"I was right there next to him. The nigga still robbed me after he shot him."

"What the fuck is that on your pants? You pissed on yourself?" Snub asked as he glared.

"Nah, I had to piss bad as hell. I thought I was pissing in the bushes, but that shit was dripping on my pants," Will muttered.

"Do BG mother know he got shot?" Snub asked, getting back to the topic.

"Yeah, she was there before the ambulance. I don't know how she found out though."

"Aight, go home and change ya pants, then meet me in the hood. I'm bout to call the homies so we can have a meeting."

"Aight, I'ma meet you in the hood," Will said before leaving.

* * * * *

Back at Mally G's house:

The sight of the gun made Mally G jump, he quickly pulled a P89 from under his stripped blue covers and pointed it at Jay's stomach.

"Cause I'm sleep, don't mean I'm sleeping," Mally G said before he got up to embrace his friend.

"How the fuck you get in here?"

"You know my boo gave me a key," Jay said jokingly.

"Yeah, aight," Mally G said in between laughs.

"Nah my lil homie Amod let me in. He keep asking to see my gun," Jay said in between laughs.

Jay went in his pocket, pulled out a knot of money and threw it on Mally G's bed.

"What's that for?" Mally G asked while looking confused.

"That's your money back. I caught Will and them slipping earlier. I done fucked around and had to shoot that motherfucker."

"You shot Will?" Mally G asked.

"Nah, I shot BG. I would've shot Will too, but I know you wanna handle that yourself being as though he robbed you."

"What happened? How you wind up shooting BG?" Mally G asked calmly, trying to mask his interest.

"When I was robbing them, that motherfucker tried to reach. I bet he won't reach again! Will bitch ass pissed on himself as soon as the first shot rang off. That shit was funny as hell. You better hope it ain't no piss on that money," Jay managed to say in between laughs. "Mally G, you can have that P89. Look what BG was reaching for." Jay pulled out a chrome gold plated 44 automatic and started dancing like a little kid with a big bag of candy.

"Let me see?" Mally G asked before analyzing the gun.

"What's fucking with this the same gun Will robbed me with. Yo, did BG die after you shot him?" Mally G asked out of concern.

"Damn, you act like you care about them niggas! Them niggas robbed you—fuck them niggas! If he dead, that's good. He won't be able to cross you again. Fuck them niggas!" Jay spat getting amped up.

"Damn, calm down nigga."

Mally G knew Jay had personal grudges with Snub and them and didn't even bother to explain the reason why Will robbed him or the fact that BG had nothing to do with it. He knew how Jay was. Once he disliked something, it was hard to convince him otherwise. Jay never forgave them for trying to jump him the day Mar Mar was arrested, and the fact that they're Blood only added to the hate. Jay didn't understand that Mally G had been living on High Street for seven years and being around them for so long made him grow love for them as well.

"You right, fuck 'em," Mally G said to avoid an argument.

"Bruh, you think your mother a let me stay here for a couple of weeks?" Jay asked.

"I don't know. Why you ask that?" Mally G asked with a puzzled look.

"When I went home this morning Karen said the cops came by looking for me over ol' boy I pistol whipped. I don't know how the fuck they know I did that shit. I think Karen might've told somebody. She said that she ain't say nothing, but I don't believe her."

"So, what you plan on doing now?" Mally G asked.

"Nigga, you could call me NORE until they catch me, Nigga On the Run Eating," Jay said as he flashed a knot of money.

"Aight, check this out. Go and pack ya shit and bring it over. I'm not gone tell my mother cause she might be on some bullshit. She work at night so she'll never know you staying here. It'll look like you just came over bout time she come home from work. We just gotta keep it from my lil brother. Amod lil ass talk too damn much."

"Aight, I'm about to go grab my shit right now. I'll be right back," Jay said before he shook Mally G's hand and left.

After Jay was gone Mally G laid in his bed and went into deep thought. *Damn, shit about to be crazy! Why did Jay have to get involved with that gang shit? If niggas bring that bullshit to my house, I'ma have no choice but to go all out. I hope Snub could keep shit peaceful until Jay find another spot to live. Nah, Snub on some bullshit too. This ain't gone work. What if that nigga Str8 Lace give another call? I gotta kill that nigga. Fuck that! Matter of fact, I'ma holla at Shice. I know he can control them cause he brought that Blood shit out here. Yeah, he a give Jay a pass. He watched us grow up! Well hopefully...*

His mother's voice brought him back to reality.

"Jamal!" Amirrah yelled from her room.

"Huh, ma!"

"I need you to go to the store and get me a philly and some cereal for your brother in the morning."

"Aight, I already got a du—" he caught himself before saying "dutch." He didn't think his mother knew he smoked.

"Oh, you already got a dutch, huh! You ain't gotta hide nothing from me, Jamal. I been knew you smoked. I found that ashtray under your dresser when I was cleaning up, and I smelled reefer when I was going to the bathroom one night."

Mally G felt relieved after hearing his mother respond so cool.

"Look, Jamal," she said as she approached his room. "I don't mind you smoking reefer as long as you stay in school and don't get caught up with all that bullshit in the streets. You probably think I worked my whole life cause I changed before you were born, but I was in the streets when I was younger too. Back in my days, everything was different though. We had gangs too. I was in the Lolly Pop gang. We use to beef with the Avenues. We had fun though. We wasn't about killing each other back then. You could fight somebody and chill with him or her the very next day. Y'all wanna kill each other as soon as somebody loses a fight.

"Jamal, just make sure you're careful out there and remember all you have is your family at the end of the day. Your friends ain't your friends, Jamal. I had to learn the hard way, learn from my mistakes. Before your father got his life sentence all his so-called friends was acting like they were there for him. Now I get letters from him telling me how everybody shitted on him and how he wish he put his family first when he was free. It's sad but there's no love in these streets. But look, go get that dutch. I had a hard day at work today. I gotta smoke."

After Mally G came back with the dutch his mother asked him if he wanted to smoke. To his surprise, Amirrah pulled out a bag of hydro.

"Ma, what you know about dro?" Mally G said in between laughs.

"Boy, I told you I was in the streets before you was thought about. Here boy, roll up cause them dutch's be falling apart. That's why I mess with my philly's," Amirrah said as she handed him the marijuana.

After they smoked, they talked for a couple of hours before Mally G realized Jay never came back.

"Aight, ma, I'ma talk to you later. I gotta see what's taking Jay so long to come back."

He went into his room to get his cell phone and called Jay's phone. The answering machine picked up on the first ring prompting him to call the house phone.

"Hello," a girl answered after the third ring.

"Who this?" Mally G asked puzzled.

"You don't call nobody house saying 'who this.' Who you?" she snapped.

"This Mally G. Where Jay at?"

"Oh, hey Mally, this Karen. Jay got locked up like an hour ago."

"What he get locked up for?" Mally G asked not wanting to believe what he just heard.

"They locked him up for a gun and for beating my friend's father up. I feel so bad. It's all my fault. Unique promised me she wasn't gone tell nobody, and she lied. How much time he gone get?" she asked as she began to cry.

"Karen, I don't know. Hopefully not much."

"Mally, he got another gun in his drawer, a big silver one and some drugs. If you could, can you come and get this stuff before my mother find it and wind up selling the gun and doing the drugs?"

"Aight, put everything in a bag. I'm on my way right now."

Chapter 4: Mally Rises

The next day:

Mally G was still in a distorted state of mind. He just didn't want to accept the fact that his best friend was incarcerated. He made plans to sell the drugs he got from Karen and get Jay the best lawyer he could find.

As Mally G was walking to the Chinese store on High Street and Clinton Avenue, he saw Shice, Snub, Menace, and Will sitting on crates in front of the Riviera Hotel from a distance. As he got closer, a guy with a black hood over his head exited a gray Cherokee sport that was double parked in the street. Shice and the others were so deep into their conversation that they didn't acknowledge the masked man until it was too late. The guy drew a Tec Nine from under his sweat hood that was hanging from a shoestring tied around his neck.

"Don't nobody move!" the guy commanded. "Put your hands against the wall!" he yelled while waving the gun motioning for them to put their hands on the Riviera Hotel's brick wall.

Mally G ducked behind a car while pulling out his P89. He crept from car to car, getting closer and closer to the encounter. Moments later, he found himself two inches behind the gunman. The guy was so occupied in searching their pockets that he didn't notice Mally G walking up on him. He placed the barrel of his P89 against the guy's hood and squeezed a bullet directly into his skull. After the guy collapsed, Mally G walked over the man's lifeless body and let off sixteen more shots into his head, causing his brain to splash all over the concrete. He squeezed the trigger five more times after the gun was already empty, causing the gun to click as the hammer was stuck back.

It felt as though some of the stress he felt was released. He'd been curious along time about how taking a person's life felt and after experiencing it, he realized it made him feel powerful. He didn't feel a bit of guilt or let it linger on his conscious. It felt so natural and, for a moment, Mally G felt a sense of pride.

Mally G walked off without saying a word to Shice or the others. The fact that he didn't run or act worried made them view him very differently. They realized then that he was ruthless.

Moments later, the scene was blocked off with the familiar yellow caution tape from the corner of Muhammad Ali Avenue and High Street to the corner of Clinton Avenue. A crowd of nosey neighbors crowded around the crime scene trying to find out what happened, and the homicide detectives showed little emotion as they did the same. The body was barely covered with a white sheet and the ambulance left just as fast as they came. Shice and the others were standing on the opposite side of the street watching the scene as they were talking quietly about what they had just witnessed.

"That's crazy," Snub said laughing while looking up the street. The rest of their eyes went in the direction Snub was looking and saw Mally G walking down from the top of High Street. He had changed his clothes and put a baseball cap over his short dread locks. He walked into the crowd and started asking questions as if he was a nosey neighbor himself. Although there was speculation, nobody knew what happened and that's all he was concerned about.

"Mally G, come here!" Snub yelled from across the street while waving his hand motioning for him to come.

When Mally G approached them, he shook all their hands before Shice said, "Yo, you shot the fuck out!"

"Why you say that?" Mally G asked with an innocent look on his face.

"That's exactly why I like ya little ass," Shice said in between laughter.

"Snub told me he spoke to you about joining the family and about that bullshit Str8 Lace did. So I spoke to Str8 Lace and he ain't know you was my lil man. You ain't gotta worry about no shit like that happening again. Mal, you know niggas fuck with you heavy, and we gone ride with you regardless. You need to fuck with the team."

"Shice, I'm saying I already fuck with y'all, but I'm not into that red versus blue shit. You already know me and Jay been best friends for as long as I could remember. I'll feel fake if I cross Jay like that, plus the only color I'm about is that green."

"I feel you, lil bruh. What you do to keep ya stomach full?" Shice asked.

"I got a few grams of crack I'm try'na get rid of now, but I don't have no certain hustle. Whatever brings in money, I'm with it."

"Aight look, being as though you put work in for the hood, you got the green light to pump that crack and when you finish holla at me when you ready to flip. You gone be the only neutral nigga out here with ya own shit as long as you copping weight from me, so you better take advantage. I know how you feel about Jay, so I'm not gone pressure you into turning Blood, but you have to keep him out our hood if you know what's best for him," Shice said.

Little did Shice know, Mally G had intentions on selling his crack regardless, but the green light made everything much better.

"Jay got bagged the other day, so you don't have to worry about him for now. But what's good with BG? Is he good?" Mally asked.

"Oh, he good. It's gone take a little time for him to heal."

Snub said knowing BG was lucky for surviving seven shots at close range.

"Did y'all ever find out who did that shit?"

"Nah, the nigga was masked up, and Will was so busy pissing on himself he ain't see where the nigga ran to," Snub said before everyone started laughing except Will.

"Fuck you, nigga! I ain't piss on myself."

"Motherfuckers must think y'all soft up here cause nigga's just keep try'na rob y'all. They know not to come on Astor Street with that shit," Menace stated.

"Nigga, you better look across the street," Snub said while nodding his head towards the crime scene. "Niggas ain't gone be try'na rob us no more, especially now that we got our new Tec Nines that nigga over there donated," he added with a smile.

"Yo, let's go to Studio Seven and get a couple drinks. All these cops that's pulling up is starting to creep me out," Shice said before walking off as everybody followed his lead.

★★★★★

"What you drinking on, lil nigga?" Shice asked Mally G as they took seats around the crowded bar.

"I don't really fuck with liquor like that. Where the weed at?"

"I can't fuck with the bali. I'm still on parole."

"Oh, aight. Fuck it. I'll drink with you, big bruh. Get me whatever you drinking," Mally G said as he scooted in his seat and nodded towards the bartender.

"Ya lil ass gone be twisted, I fuck with the murda juice. Mami, give me two cups of Bacardi 151 with coke. No! The big red cups!" Shice yelled at the bartender as he saw her reaching towards small clear cups.

When the bartender put Mally G's second cup in front of him, he was already wasted from the first. He walked over to the karaoke machine by the back of the bar and inserted his money while trying to keep his composure. Three girls walked into the bar as he was looking for a song to play.

"Ma, come here!" he said as he motioned for one of the girls to come to him.

"Who, me?" one of the girls said before looking over both of her shoulders while pointing to her chest.

"Yeah, you," he said while nodding his head up and down. "What's your name, cutie?" Mally G asked when she approached him.

"My name is Zakia, but everybody calls me ZaZa. What's your name?" she replied in a gentle voice.

"Jamal but everybody call me Mally G," he spoke while smiling and looking into her eyes. "I called you over here so you could pick the song we gone have our first dance to."

"How you know if I wanna dance with you?" ZaZa said in a soft and sweet voice.

"Cause I know you," Mally G winked.

"Where you know me from?" She asked with an expression full of confusion.

"I got a time machine. You my future wife," Mally G said with a grin.

"Boy, you crazy. Put on Real Love by Mary J. Blige, that jawn go hard," ZaZa said before her friends came over and one handed her a cranberry and vodka.

"Where y'all from?"

"We from Philly, but my friend Tammy lives in East Orange now," ZaZa answered.

"What got y'all around here then?" Mally G asked.

"Tammy works at the Rite Aid across the street. This was her idea to come in here."

"Which one is Tammy? I gotta buy her a drink for bringing you in my life," Mally G said before a bright smile appeared across his face.

"Boy, you is crazy," ZaZa said in between laughs while pointing to the girl that gave her the drink. Mally G brought all of them drinks before him and ZaZa started to dance. He was drunk, and the liquor made her look extra exotic along with the fact that she could dance.

ZaZa was beyond gorgeous. She was 5'6, just a little shorter than Mally G and about 130 pounds. She was slim, but thick in all the right places, accentuating her nice plump butt with a mean cuff. She had a hand full of breast that sat up perfect, long straight hair that came a little below her shoulders, and a caramel complexion that glowed off her body. She had chinky eyes that accented her bright smile with dimples and nice juicy lips with gloss on them making them look even more luscious. ZaZa's looks hypnotized Mally G.

She was slowly grinding her soft plump butt on his manhood. Her body fragrance drove him crazy. She was so soft and smelled like she just got out of the shower seconds ago.

He had his hands on her hips dancing along as he spoke to her in her ear, "Where you going when you leave here?"

"I'm staying at Tammy's house tonight. So, I guess I'm going there."

"You might as well stay with me tonight."

"I just met you. Boy, you really crazy," she uttered as she pushed her butt harder against his jeans.

He turned her around until they were face to face, and he could feel her breath against his lips. "Look, ma, I know we just met but the vibe I get from you it seems like I knew you forever. Trust me, I won't hurt you and I'll never make you do something you don't want to do. My night been so good so far, but it would be perfect if I could end it with you. Don't look at me as a stranger; look at me as a friend you just met. This is the beginning of our friendship and hopefully in the future you will be mine. Sometimes you have to take risks in life. I promise you, you won't regret it," he said with his best innocent look.

"My gut feeling telling me I could trust you. It's something about you. Where you live at?"

"I live around the corner on High Street."

"Aight, if anything my home girl gone drop us off so she could know where I'm staying, and don't think we having sex either cause I don't get down like that," she stated as she slightly backed away to give him a stern look.

"That's not a problem. I just wanna end my night with you. You sleeping in the same bed while I hold you is enough to turn my good night great, and waking up to your pretty face is a bonus," he assured her.

"Aight, I'll be right back," she said as she walked off towards her friends.

Mally G knew once he got her in his house that getting her to have sex would be the easy part. He had a way with words when it came to convincing girls to have sex with him. He was a pro at one-night stands. He never really been in an official relationship but dealt with many girls in his life. He considered himself a mac and never wanted to settle down, but lately he was realizing that being a mac meant being lonely. Having sex with a girl is one thing but being emotionally attached was something he had never had before. He felt as though he had not found the right one yet, but he had a feeling he would find her soon. He was curious about finding out what all the talk about being in love was really about. ZaZa definitely was wifey potential, but Mally G didn't know if she really looked that good to him or if the liquor was playing tricks on him.

★★★★★

Tammy's green Toyota Celica came to a halt in front of Mally G's house before him and ZaZa exited.

"ZaZa, make sure you call me as soon as you wake up and don't do nothing I wouldn't do," Tammy yelled as they walked towards Mally G's house.

"Shut up girl. Y'all be safe driving home. Love y'all!" ZaZa yelled.

"Love you too! Mally G take care of my sister," Tammy said while pulling off.

"She in good hands. Don't worry!" Mally G yelled back.

Once they walked in the house, they went straight up the stairs to his room while trying to keep quiet. Mally G sat on the bed while ZaZa stood there looking at the pictures he had on his wall. He had a collage of pictures of himself, his little brother, and his friends taped on his wall. He had a lot of solo pictures he took on special occasions when he went out.

"Let me get this picture? You look so cute right here," ZaZa said while pointing to a picture of him standing outside that was taken last Easter.

"If I give you that picture, it's gone mess up my whole set up. I got you. I'ma give you a different picture. And what you mean I'm cute in that picture? I'm cute in all my pictures," he said jokingly as he laid back and kicked off his shoes.

"Before I get comfortable, do you want something to drink or eat?"

"No, I'm okay but thank you anyway," ZaZa replied politely.

Once she finished looking at his pictures, she kicked off her black sneakers with silver laces and laid down next to him on the bed. They started watching television, and then Mally G went off into deep thought. *Damn, this bitch bad. I hope she ain't on no bullshit cause I'm drunk as hell.* He felt the liquor taking a toll on him, as his eyes were getting heavier. *Hell no! Let me get up before I blow my night by falling asleep.*

He leaned over clasping his hand around her neck and kissed her softly on the lips to see how she would react. ZaZa started kissing him back enticing him. He got on top of her taking control of the situation. The taste of alcohol on her breath made him feel as though he had a better chance. He went from her lips up to her ear breathing harder as he kissed her earlobes making her body shiver. He knew she was getting horny by her body language, but he wanted to get her to the max before he went in for the kill.

After about five more minutes of kissing her delicately and pushing up against her warm body, he tried to unfasten her belt buckle. She put her hand over his and stopped him.

"No, baby. We can't."

"Why, what's wrong?" Mally G asked in a whining tone.

"Cause we just met today. I have respect for myself, I'm not like that."

"Damn girl you don't know how you got me feeling right now. You got me horny as hell."

"I'm sorry. I ain't mean to tease you. I just love kissing and since my last relationship, I haven't had nobody to kiss. It been so long. I'm sorry," she replied as though she knew she disappointed him.

After Mally G sat in silence for a moment he leaned back on top of her and began kissing her again now that he knew kissing was her weakness. His motive was to get her horny until she couldn't resist it anymore. He started off kissing her on the lips softly as she kissed him back. He rubbed his stiff dick against her pussy as he passionately kissed her, causing her body to shiver once again. He started kissing down her neck as he lifted her shirt up exposing her perfect breasts. He unfastened her bra and began to lick all around her erect nipples. Then, he began flicking his tongue up and down her nipples, causing her to squirm as light moans escaped her mouth. In his mind, he knew she was too horny to turn back, so he reached for her belt buckle again. Just as the first time, she put her hand over his stopping him again.

"I can't," she said in a low tone knowing she wanted to.

"Come on, baby. You know you want it just as bad as me."

"You right. I do want it just as bad as you, but I can't. We just met."

"So you saying if we knew each other longer it would have been different?"

"Of course."

"What? You think if we have sex tonight, I'ma get the pussy and try to play you after that?"

"I don't know and that's what scares me. I don't wanna be used. I don't want to give myself to you and wind up hurting myself in the long run. Also, as a woman I have morals. I still can't believe I came over here with you. I just can't see myself having sex with a guy I only knew for a few hours. It's not you, it's me."

Mally G looked into her eyes before saying, "ZaZa, I already have respect for you. I'm one hundred percent sure I got you horny as hell and you didn't give in. I respect you for having control of your hormones. Now I know once you're mine another nigga can't get you horny and take advantage of you.

"ZaZa, you do something special to me, chills ran through my body when we were kissing. It's something about you that make me feel like this is where I belong. But let me explain something to you. I could act like I want a relationship with you for a few months, but my main intention could be just to have sex with you. Then, by the time we have sex, you'll have more feelings for me and you would be crushed when you find out my real intentions. So knowing a person for a few months don't mean you really know them. Just know, if we have sex tonight or if we don't, you gonna see that I'ma be the same nigga tomorrow.

"And let's just say if I was to be on some bullshit and try to play you, which I won't, you won't be so hurt cause your feelings wasn't involved. I'm really feeling you. Don't look at it as you're giving it up on the first night, look at it as the beginning of our future. I know you're not a hoe and you know it too, so let's not base our actions on morals that don't mean a damn thing! ZaZa, you good, just trust me, I won't let you down," Mally G said before he unfastened her belt.

Once he got her zipper down, he knew the door to heaven was open, but he didn't rush in. He took her shirt off and tossed it on the floor, then took his off and did the same. He started kissing her softly on her lips, then worked his way down to her breasts, licking around her nipples, teasing her before placing one in his mouth while sucking it gently. She lightly moaned, as her pussy got wetter making her panties moist.

"Come on, Mally. I'm ready. I want you inside of me," ZaZa moaned before removing the remainder of her clothes.

He stripped down naked with the exception of his socks and put on a magnum condom he pulled out of his back pocket. She laid on her back, then he climbed on top of her. She opened her legs wider, and then wrapped her arms around his neck as she felt his manhood entering her wet pussy.

"Go slow, okay…" she flinched as his head slowly entered. She put her hand on his stomach to stop him from going in too fast.

Damn this shit tight and wet as hell. This too good to be true, Mally G thought to himself.

"Ahhhh!!" ZaZa moaned while lightly biting her bottom lip as he put the full length into her.

He held his upper body up in a push up position while sliding in and out of her in a slow pace. He couldn't believe how firm her pussy was around his dick. After a few minutes, he picked up his pace while her moans grew louder and louder.

"Uhhhh! Uhhhh! Ahhhh! Mal…aally!!!" she whimpered.

After a few minutes he lifted her legs up, then pushed them back as far as they could go and began to long stroke her. She held her breath every time he pushed in, feeling his dick pushing against her walls going in her stomach. Her juices were dripping down her crack making her asshole and the sheets soaked. Her pussy started making a slurping sound as juices escaped. *Damn this shit wet as hell*! Mally G thought after feeling the wetness on his pubic hairs.

He picked up his pace as she began moaning louder now from painful pleasure. "Uhhh! Maa…all…ally! Ahhhh! Don't stop…Please!" He started pumping faster. "Uh! Uh! Uh! Uh! Uhhhh!!! Please don't stop, baby!!! Please don't stop!! Ohhh!"

She moaned out as he kissed her earlobes and whispered, "You know you almost made me miss this." He started pumping harder and faster.

"Uh! Uh! I'm sorry, oh my God!! I'm sorry!" she cried as he pounded her pussy. "Ohh!! Oh! I'm cumming!" she shouted before she threw her head back. Suddenly her body stiffened. She wrapped her legs around him stopping him from pumping. "Oohh!" Her whole body vibrated as her juices overflowed leaving a puddle on the sheets. He couldn't believe how wet she was.

"Turn over," he said breathing heavily.

Seconds later he had her on her hands and knees. He got off the bed and stood up behind her while she arched her back leaving her ass tooted in the air. He leaned down and kissed her on her lower back an inch above her butt, causing chills to run up her spine. He entered her slowly from behind. She began to moan as soon as he entered her.

"Uhhh... Uhhh! Ahhh!" Her moans grew louder as he picked up the pace. "Ahhh... Aaaahhhhh... Ohhh!" Her butt lightly jiggled each time their bodies met. He realized she was a squirter when her body tensed and her vagina started spitting like a super soaker. "Ahhh... Ahhh... Uhh baby! Please nut, baby, ohhh! I can't take no more!" she moaned.

As he was pumping, he wrapped his arms around her legs and lifted her in the air leaving only her hands on the bed. Now he had full control over her body. He squeezed his dick muscles and began pumping harder and faster, guiding her body into his trying to get himself to nut.

Sweat was dripping down his face as she continued to moan loud enough to wake up the dead. "Uhhh... Uhhh... Uhh!! Ohh…my…god! Oh! Oh! Oh... Mally! Ohhhh! I'm bout to nut again! Ohhhh!" she yelled as her pussy tightened around his erection. He pushed into her as far as he could as they both orgasmed simultaneously. Both of them weakened as chills ran through their bodies. He threw her on the bed and she was still moaning as if he was still in her. "Uhhh… Uhh… Uhhh!" she moaned before silencing.

He put on his boxers and went in the bathroom to flush the condom and clean himself up. He was still a little drunk as he looked in the mirror and spoke to himself in a low tone. "Nigga, you beat that pussy up, you a beast." He looked down at his dick and said, "you know how to get the job done… my nigga," then chuckled before exiting the bathroom.

Chapter 5: Confusion

One week later:

"Damn! Mally G, you out here early as hell," Snub said while approaching him from the street.

"Yeah man, I gotta get this money right. I got a couple weeks left before school start back, so I gotta work full time while I still got the chance," Mally G said before handing a fiend a dime of crack cocaine.

"Yo! You got that shit in your pocket?" Snub asked after seeing Mally G stuff something in his pocket.

"Yeah man, I ain't beat for running back and forth from no stash."

"You gotta put that shit in the oven," Snub said as he reached his hand behind him pretending to shove something in his butt while laughing.

"My ass only got an exit door," Mally G said while frowning.

"Nigga, you ain't gotta put it in ya asshole, you put it between ya cheeks."

"Fuck all that! My cheeks little as fuck. I'm keeping it right in my pocket. What's the point of me stashing my drugs when I got this with me?" Mally G said while lifting his t-shirt revealing his gun.

"Yo, you wilding! You still carrying that ratchet knowing it got a body on it?"

"Nah, this a different one. I got rid of that dirty one yesterday. I love these shits! When you miss all five shots out of that revolver, I got twelve more shots for that ass." Mally G paused for a moment then continued, "Yo, Snub, on some real shit I think I know who shot BG…"

"Ay, nephew, you got dimes?" an addict interrupted while scratching her arm.

"Yeah, how many you want?" Mally G asked before pulling out his bag of drugs.

"Can I talk to you on the side?"

"Whatever you gotta say, just say it! It's not gonna make a difference if we on the side or not," Mally G said, while sounding aggravated.

"Look, I got this white dude at my house he scared to come around here. I saw him counting a lot of money. He wanna make sure the shit good before he start spending his money. Once he get started. he gone spend all that shit. I came to y'all cause I fuck with y'all. Just give me a dime, and I'll be right back."

"Get the fuck out of here with that bullshit game! If you would've just asked and said you was fucked up, I probably would've gave you one. You fucked up now. Get the fuck out of here!" She put her head down and put on a sad face before walking away. "Now what you was saying about you know who shot BG?"

"Oh yeah, I wasn't trying to get in between y'all Blood shit, but I fuck with BG. A bitch told me she heard one of your homies bragging about that shit."

"Who? What homie?" Snub asked impatiently.

"Look you can't say nothing cause he got high status, and I gotta ask the bitch more questions to solidify it." He got silent for a moment then continued, "Str8 Lace."

"Word! I knew it was something funny about that dude. And my status higher than his now so that high status shit don't mean nothing. Holla at that bitch a.s.a.p. and get at me!" Snub said with an aggressive tone.

"Say no more. I got you as soon as I holla at her."

"Mally G, you know we throwing a welcome home party at the Play House for my lil brother when he come home," Snub said, changing the subject.

"Word! When lil bruh get out?"

"His trial suppose to start next month, but they don't got shit on him. The nigga that got poked up girl said she saw the whole thing and Mar Mar ain't do it. The only charge that's gonna stick is the receiving stolen property, and he gon' get time served for that shit."

"That's what's good. Yo, take me downtown so I could start getting my school clothes," Mally G said, before he took a wad of money out of his pocket and started counting.

"Come on," Snub said as he began to walk toward his car.

"Nah, not right now. As soon as I get rid of this little bit of shit," Mally G said before he took out a little plastic bag and shook it to see how many dimes he had left.

★★★★★

Snub pulled up downtown and parked his Ford Taurus in the parking lot on Halsey Street with Mally G in the passenger side. It was 1:00 pm, and downtown was crowded. Bootleggers were in front of almost every store selling fake DVD's, CD's, sneakers, pocketbooks, and anything else they could hustle for some cash. There was a crowd of young kids standing in front of the pizza store on Broad and Market crowding around two young boys dancing to club music coming from the CD stand next to the store.

"Go Mally! Go Mally! Go Mally!" Snub sung, trying to soup Mally G up to dance as they walked past.

Mally G stopped, moved his arm as if he was about to bust some dance moves then said "get the fuck out of here!" while laughing.

They crossed the street and entered the Source. Snub picked up a pair of black, white and red Huarache Nikes before saying, "These shits go hard!"

"Damn! I never seen nobody with them," Mally G said before he grabbed the sneaker out of Snub's hand and analyzed it. "I'm copping these," Mally G said before he waved an employee over to help.

"How you gonna try and cop the sneakers I wanted?" Snub said with a frown.

"Them shits dope, and I never saw nobody with them. I can't let nobody in da hood get them first. You can get them too," Mally G said as he pulled out the money to pay for his sneakers.

"I don't want them now. I'm not try'na look like ya twin," Snub said while shaking his head side to side.

When they left out the store, Mally G handed Snub his bags and said, "Here, take this to the car. I'm bout to run around the corner on Branford and get us some uptowns."

"Make sure they don't put all that ice in my shit. It barely be something to drink in them cups!"

"Aight, I got you," Mally G said before walking away.

As Mally G was walking, a Jamaican guy gave him a cold stare causing him to feel uncomfortable. *What the fuck did I do to him*? he thought after catching eye contact with the Rasta.

"Watch yourself, mon!" the guy yelled while looking directly at Mally G.

"What the fuck you mean watch myself?" Mally G yelled back as he reached for his gun and started walking towards him.

"You no kill me, mon! You need me!" the Rasta said, sounding confident as he slapped his hands on his chest. Mally G was confused. He had no idea what the Rasta was talking about. "Something bad soon to come!" the Rasta said with his left hand on a necklace hanging from his neck that looked like it was made of rat bones.

"What the fuck is you talking about?" Mally G snapped, getting frustrated.

"Mon, place you hand on de necklace. Me read you future."

Mally G started to walk off then he thought, *What if something bad is really gone happen. Maybe I could change my future if I knew it.*

"Aight, how I'm gone know if what your telling me is the truth?"

"Touch de Ankh and you see!"

Mally G wrapped his hand around the medallion that was connected to the bones, which looked like a cross with a circle at the top. The Rasta rubbed some kind of oil on the center of his forehead, lit a black candle, and mumbled a few words Mally G didn't understand before he began talking.

"You lost your main road dawg only for now. When he return, he trust no more. You heart is cold as ice. I see you no trust people. You trust a gyal soon."

"I see you know a little about me, but what's bad that's gonna happen? Fuck all the bullshit!" Mally G said, cutting him off as he was getting impatient again.

"See, mon, me getting there now. I see you getting shot."

"What! You said I'ma get shot?" Mally G asked really not wanting to believe what he had just heard. "When I'm getting shot? Am I gonna die?" he asked the Rasta not really wanting to know the answer.

"No! No! Mon, you no die. You get shot in de leg," he replied still holding on to his necklace.

"Who the fuck gone shoot me? When I'ma get shot? Where my friends gone be at? Can I stop it? Am—"

"Hold! Hold, mon!" he yelled. "Me answer you. You get shot at 5 o'clock today. De shooter wear jersey number 5, and you friends laugh at you. Oh, one more thing. He has locs like you," the Rasta said while looking directly into Mally G's eyes.

Mally G had heard enough. He let go of the necklace and walked off in deep thoughts. *Damn! This some crazy shit. I ain't getting shot at no 5 o'clock. Fuck that! I'll kill every nigga I see wearing a jersey with the number 5 on it. I need to get high. This some bullshit.*

Mally G walked straight back to the car. When he got in, Snub realized he didn't have his iced tea mixed with lemonade.

"You took all that fucking time and gone come back empty handed! What the fuck happened to our uptowns?"

"Man, I don't even want to talk about it," Mally G said as he lowered his head while shaking it from side to side.

"Man, what the fuck happened! I don't wanna hear that I don't wanna talk about it shit either! You better tell me something. Had me waiting in this hot ass car for nothing."

"Man, this fucking Rasta dude read my future and told me some bullshit!"

Snub bust out into laughter, "Man, that shit fake. You sitting over there about to cry like a bitch over some fake voodoo." He held his stomach as he bursted into tears again.

"Whatever, man. This shit ain't funny! Take me home!" Mally G said still looking serious.

He was quiet the rest of the ride home thinking about his encounter with the Rasta. *That motherfucker gotta be telling the truth. He said I lost my main road dawg and that I don't trust people. Jay did get locked up, and I always had a problem trusting people. Damn, he right! Plus, he said I will soon trust a girl, and I do kind of trust ZaZa. But why the fuck would niggas laugh about me getting shot, and why wouldn't Jay trust me no more? This shit crazy!*

When he went in the house, he put on his bulletproof vest and tucked the gold plated 44 automatic into his waistline next to his P89. He was determined to kill whoever he thought was going to shoot him in order to change his future. He kept pacing back and forth in his room thinking about what he was going to do next. His thoughts were racing. *Yo this shit crazy. I should just keep my ass in the house. Nah then if nothing happen Snub gone tease me forever. Fuck it! I ain't no bitch, I got two straps and a vest I'm ready for whatever! I gotta smoke another blunt.*

He decided to walk to the liquor store to get a bottle and some cigars for his weed. Once he came out the liquor store on High and Spruce, he sat on the edge of the brick porch of building #730 and began drinking.

He drank a half pint of Hennessy and smoked a blunt by himself. Mally G was beyond high and drunk—he was wasted. His mind was racing so much he didn't notice how much liquor he had drunk. The weed only made the situation worst.

Snub, Shice, Menace and Str8 Lace pulled up in Str8 Lace's Civic, and they all got out and walked towards Mally G. He looked to see if any of them had on a jersey, but none of them did. He pulled his phone out of his pocket and the screen read 4:00 pm. *Damn! One more hour,* he thought before letting out a light chuckle.

"Lil bruh, what's good?" Shice said before extending his arm to him.

"Chilling, man," Mally G slurred as he shook Shice's hand.

"Damn, Mally G you cooking early, huh," Menace said analyzing him while laughing.

"I know you ain't still bugging over that fortune telling shit," Snub said while looking for a response.

"I'm good," Mally G slurred, sounding the complete opposite.

"Big bruh, come on let's bust that move. Finisher just called me," Str8 Lace said to Shice.

"Lil bruh, come take this ride with me. You too fucked up to be standing out here. Plus, I gotta holla at you about something," Shice said as he put his arm around Mally G and started walking towards Str8 Lace Civic.

Shice got in the passenger seat while Mally G and Snub jumped in the back. "Menace, we bumming right back!" he yelled out the window before Str8 Lace pulled off.

"Trillz!" Menace replied back.

Moments later, they pulled up in front of building #440 on Elizabeth Avenue. Str8 Lace and Snub got out and walked in the building.

"Mally G, did you ever holla at ol girl that overheard Str8 Lace bragging about robbing BG and them?"

Mally G was looking confused. The liquor took a toll on him, and the question caught him off guard.

"Yeah, Snub told me about it," Shice said with a smile on his face.

"Nah, I ain't even holla at that bitch yet," Mally G said while rubbing his hands down his face trying to get focused.

"Damn! I gotta piss like a racehorse!" Shice said before getting out the car and walking towards a tree.

Mally G mind was racing, and he knew he had to react fast if he wanted his plan to work. He didn't expect Snub to tell Shice so fast, but now was the perfect opportunity to while they were in Str8 Lace car. He looked around first, then pulled the gold plated 44 automatic from his waistline and placed it in Str8 Lace's armrest next to a book of CD's.

Snub, Str8 Lace, and Shice were all approaching the car around the same time as Mally G looked up. Snub and Shice got right into the car. Meanwhile, Str8 Lace opened his door, pressed the button to open the trunk, and then proceeded to the rear of the car.

"Shice, put in a different CD. I'm tired of listening to the same shit," Mally G said.

"Snub, where he keep his CDs?"

"Check the armrest," Mally G suggested. As soon as he opened the armrest, he noticed the gold plated 44 and frowned his face. "Snub, ain't this the gun that BG got robbed for?"

"Hell yeah! Let me see," Snub said before looking it over in awe. "Yeah, this definitely it. I remember this broke safety button. That bitch was telling Mally G the truth then cause the nigga that robbed him took this gun."

Before anybody could say another word, Mally G spoke up. "Fuck that! Let me handle that nigga, Shice. He a fucking snake. Plus, he made Will rob me!"

Mally G grabbed the 44 out of Snub's hand and got out of the car without getting the okay. Because Shice didn't try to stop him, he proceeded to walk up to Str8 Lace just as the trunk was closing. When he raised the gun to Str8 Lace's face, he was clueless to what was going on.

"Why you make Will rob me, you bitch ass motherfucker?" Mally G slurred while looking him directly in his eyes. Before Str8 Lace could utter a word **POW!!** A bullet was entering his forehead and just as quick two more followed the first one. **POW!! POW!!** The gun jammed before the fourth bullet made it into the chamber.

Frightened by the loud sound of the gunshots, a crowd of people scattered in all directions.

When Mally G jumped back in the car he realized that Shice was already in the driver's seat. He looked at the clock on the dashboard and it read 4:59pm. He looked back and saw three guys running towards the car from behind. Two of the three guys appeared to have on jerseys, but Mally G couldn't see what numbers were on them. As they were running closer, he realized one of the two had dread locs.

That gotta be the nigga that's gonna shoot me. I'ma get that motherfucker first! Mally G thought as he reached for his P89. Panicking while drunk, he tried to pull on his gun handle. His finger pressed the trigger as it got caught between his pants and belt.

POW!!!

He couldn't believe what just happened as he felt a burn and warm blood running down his leg. He shot himself. In a daze, he looked down and noticed he had on a jersey with the number 5 on it. He looked up at the clock and 5:00 pm was lit up on the dash.

Damn!

Chapter 6: The Heat is On

Two weeks later:

Mally G was lucky enough to recover fast. The bullet went in and out, missing his bone. It ended up being a minor injury.

He stayed in the house most of the time healing while ZaZa kept him company. They had been spending a lot of time together since they met. Mally G felt like he finally found the girl he had been looking for his entire life. Their bond was strong. He felt like he could talk to her about anything, and she understood him. He never spoke to her about his street life, and she never asked. She gave him his space but also made sure she was always there when he needed her. It was only three months since they met, but it seemed like they had known each other forever.

Mally G's bond with Menace also grew stronger as the days went on. They had been hustling and hanging out together all the time. They both went to Malcolm X Shabazz High School and would walk to school together.

One day as they were walking to school, a gray 300zx pulled alongside of them and a guy yelled, "Yo! You slob now?" Then he shaped his hand like a gun, pointed it at Mally G, and jerked it back as if a bullet came out of it.

"I gotta get a g-ride. This walking shit ain't gone cut it. I can't be slipping like this!" Mally G said as he looked at the 300zx from a distance.

Everybody was assuming that Mally G was Blood now being as though he hung around them all the time. He had also bought a couple of red shirts and hats to match the red, black, and white Huarache Nikes he bought. That made him look like a Blood even more. He was hanging around them so often that he found himself talking like them as well. He was beginning to use words such as "trillz" and "bali." When Bloods from other blocks would come on High Street, they would always try to peace him thinking he was Blood. He would always have to pull his hand back and explain to them that he wasn't gang banging. At the same time, he hated when Shice, Snub, Will, BG, or Menace would excuse him to talk about Blood information. It made him feel like he wasn't a part of the team.

★★★★★

It was Friday, and Mar Mar's welcome home party was later that night. Snub came to pick Mally G and Menace up from school.

"Hurry the fuck up!" Snub yelled.

Mally G ignored him and continued talking to a girl by the front of the school building. Cars behind Snub began honking their horns because he was double-parked.

"Motherfucker, wait!" Mally G yelled while walking towards the car.

"That red look good, Blood!" Snub said to Mally G while laughing.

"Yeah aight! I'm bout to stop wearing this shit. Fucking with this red, everybody think I'm Blood. What's fucking with some crab nigga called me a slob when I was walking to school this morning and shot me with his hand. I ain't with that shit. I'm bout to start bringing the ratchet to school!"

"How you gone get it in through the metal detectors?" Menace asked.

"I'ma go in first while you wait by Mr. Bell's class window. The class be empty, and he don't got no first period class. So you could just throw the book bag up to me. You know that window low as hell." Their conversation got cut short by the sound of Mally G phone ringing.

"Hey, baby!" he said after seeing ZaZa's number.

"Hey, baby. Where you at?"

"I'm in the car with Snub. He just picked me up from school. Why, what up?"

"Baby, I want to see you. I miss you," ZaZa spoke in a whining baby tone.

"Hhmmmm! I miss you too baby, but I can't come and see you right now. We about to handle something. I'ma see you at Mar Mar party tonight. You coming, right?"

"I don't know. Tammy went down south so I don't have a ride."

"Damn! Mally G, stop boo loving. I'm try'na turn the music back up!" Snub barked.

"Look, baby. I'ma try my best to see you before the night is over with, but I'ma speak to you later, aight?"

"Aight, baby. I'ma try my best to get a ride, I really miss you. Hopefully I see you later," ZaZa said before hanging up.

"BG hit me before I picked y'all up. He said him, Will, and Mar Mar got a jump bitch at the crib. He said she trained to go. I'm bout to shoot over there and get my dick wet!" Snub said excitingly before he turned up the music and started bouncing up and down in his seat while driving faster.

★★★★★

Str8 Lace was originally from Elizabeth Avenue. Most of his family was Blood's too, but they were Gangsta Killer Bloods (G.K.B). Str8 Lace ended up turning Sex Money Murda (S.M.M.) because he was cellmates with Shice in prison, and they became real close. Str8 Lace's cousin had real high status under G.K.B. and was well respected in Newark. He tried to get Str8 Lace to change his set numerous of times, but he remained loyal to Shice and his set.

Str8 Lace's cousin was Farod, but everybody called him Finisher. He got his name from the old heads from his neighborhood. Every time there was a beef, he would always be the one to finish it by killing whoever needed to go. He never left his block until all his drugs were finished. He lived up to the name. Finisher had become furious over his little cousin's death. He believed whoever killed his family had to get finished by any means necessary.

"I saw the whole thing, Finisher. I was right there when it happened," Mango said.

"So why the fuck it take you two weeks to let me know this shit?" Finisher said with an aggressive tone.

"I was trying to handle the nigga myself then come tell you about it when I was done," Mango plead back.

"Being that you couldn't handle it yourself, tell me what da fuck you saw!"

"I saw Str8 Lace digging in his trunk when I was crossing the street coming from the park. I was about to go say 'what's up' when I saw a dude getting out of his car with a gun in his hand. I thought he was about to give it to Str8 Lace to put in the trunk, but he put it to his head. Next thing you know, he shot him."

"So you telling me the motherfucker that killed my cousin was with him?" Finisher asked while giving him a cold stare.

"Yeah! After he shot him, he got in the back seat of Str8 Lace's car and they drove off," Mango replied getting hyped.

"Str8 Lace and his homie Snub just came from picking up some weight from me. His homies said somebody did a drive by when they was walking to his car. I don't see why they would kill him. If I find out you lying, I'ma finish you!" Finisher said looking Mango in his big brown eyes with a serious serial killer stare.

"Come on, Finisher. I wouldn't lie about no shit like that. Str8 Lace was my homie too," Mango pleaded again.

"So, if you was to see the nigga again, you telling me you'll be able to recognize him?"

"Yeah! I'll never forget that nigga face!" Mango said, feeling a bit relieved.

"Aight, we'll check this out. Them niggas suppose to be having a party at the Play House tonight. Yeah, they coming to our hood, and Pete checking people at the door so you know what it is. Show me the nigga that killed my cousin, and I'ma finish his ass!" Finisher said before he pulled a 44 Bulldog from his waist, pointed it at Mango, and jerked his wrist back while saying "POW!"

★ ★ ★ ★ ★

BG and Mar Mar had just got finished gang banging the girl that BG brought to the house. BG met her through some guys he knew from school, and they told him that she was a pretty hoe that would fuck the whole block if they lined up. After they were finished taking turns fucking her and getting their dicks sucked, it was Will's turn to go in.

Will couldn't believe how pretty she was. She was a redbone with long natural hair and a cute, innocent face. Her body type was on point with the perfect set of breasts and the fattest ass Will had ever seen naked. When he walked in the room, she was laying on the bed still naked with her ass propped up in the air.

"What's ya name, sexy?" Will asked as his eyes gazed over her body.

"My name Kay, why?" She asked trying to figure out his motive.

"Nah, you pretty as hell. I want to get to know you. Where you from?" Will asked while approaching the bed.

"I'm from down the net."

"Kay, you pretty as hell. I'd love to have a wifey that look like you. Why you letting niggas do this to you?" he asked in a sincere voice.

"I don't know where you getting at, but I only get to live once. I like fucking so I fuck! I'm grown so I can do whatever I want with my body. If you wanna fuck, come on, but I'm not answering no more of ya stupid ass questions. You acting like a damn cop!" Kay sat up, aggravated by all the questions Will was asking.

"Aight, calm down, baby girl. Can I have a kiss then? I never kissed a girl pretty as you," Will moved over to Kay and began kissing her as Snub walked in.

"Oh, shit! Will in here try'na cuff! He in here kissing her! Move ya fat ass over so I could get right," Snub exclaimed.

He pulled down his pants and put his dick in her face. She immediately starting to jerk and lick the tip of his dick tasting his pre-cum. Then she put her mouth around his dick and started sucking it like it was a lollypop. Snub had a handful of her hair wrapped around his fingers as he guided her head up and down. It felt like she didn't have teeth because her mouth was so warm and wet.

Will entered her moist pussy from behind. "Mmmm!" Her moan was muffled by Snub's dick. She was going down as far as she could on his dick and popping her lips off the head when she came up. Snub was amazed at how good her head game was and the popping noise her mouth was making made it even better. She was sucking his dick like Will wasn't fucking her. His eyes started to roll into the back of his head while he leaned his head back and bit his bottom lip. Will's orgasm came in less than two minutes and then he left the room. Kay's oral sex was so good Snub continued to get head after Will left the room.

Moments later, Mally G walked in and saw her prefect round ass in the air as she was face down giving Snub oral sex.

Damn! This bitch ass fat as hell! Mally G thought as he walked closer. Snub shook his head up and down smiling.

"Go head," Snub muttered.

Mally G read Snub's lips as he nodded towards Kay. Mally put on a condom and rubbed two fingers up into her pussy which was already wet. He wasted no time entering her wetness from behind.

Damn this hoe got some good ass pussy, he thought as he smiled.

Kay moaned loud as she felt the difference, and Mally G began to pound her pussy from behind.

"Mmmmmm!! Mmmmmmm!!" she moaned with Snub's dick still muffling the sound.

Mally G speeded up and started to fuck her harder trying to make her bite Snub's dick. She couldn't take it any longer and spit Snub's dick out of her mouth as her moans escaped. Mally G's intentions were to show off so seeing Kay's reaction was a mission accomplished.

"Uhhhhh!!! Ahhhhh!!! Ohhh my God!!!"

Mally G was fucking her like she never had been fucked before. Each motion made her whole body feel numb, so she looked back to see who was fucking her so well. Her heart dropped as she looked into Mally G's eyes.

"Karen!" Mally G yelled after realizing who he was fucking.

His heart skipped a beat. He quickly pulled out and got dressed while Karen covered herself with the sheets. Tears began to run down her face. Snub was standing there with his dick in his hand looking dumb founded.

"What happened?" Snub asked.

"Karen, put ya fucking clothes on!" Mally G yelled before throwing her jeans and bra at her.

"Why you making her get dressed?" Snub asked still confused.

"This like my sister. This Jay lil sister, Karen!" he said lowering his head while shaking it from side to side still in shock.

After Karen got dressed, Mally G called her a cab and no one spoke about it. She was embarrassed and felt like she had degraded herself. She had let guys run trains on her multiple times before and never had a problem with it. Now, after going through an experience like this, it made her look at the situation in a whole different perspective. It took her to make a mistake and have sex with a person she looked at as a brother to realize how thoughtless she was about who she had sex with. Then the thought of how good Mally G felt inside her crossed her mind. *Damn!*

Chapter 7: Conflict

Later on that day:

"Mally G, ride with me to the Play House real fast?" Snub asked.

"Damn, it's early as hell. What, you try'na be the first nigga in there?"

"Nah, I gotta make sure everything is set up right. Plus, that's the only way we can get our ratchets in," Snub said before lifting his shirt half way up revealing his gun.

"Trillz! I'm bout to shoot to my house and grab my baby too. I'ma meet you at ya car," Mally G wanted to make sure he was carrying too.

"Hurry the fuck up too!" Snub yelled while Mally G walked towards his house.

They stopped at the liquor store and purchased a bottle of Bacardi 151 and ten cases of C&C can sodas in all flavors. When they pulled up to the Play House, it was 8 o'clock. They carried the bags upstairs and put everything away. The club was still empty with the exception of the owner and the DJ who was setting up his equipment.

The club was only big enough to hold about 150 people. It had a small stage and a DJ booth to the right, a small bathroom to the left, and a little juice bar off to the far-left corner that only served water and sodas.

Snub brought the sodas to sell for a dollar each to try and make some of his money back that he spent to rent the place. He had planned to sell a little bit of the liquor too, but it was mainly for him and his homies. They sat at the bar and started drinking.

Before they knew it, the club was jampacked. Snub and his homies were all drunk. Young girls were dancing with everybody, young boys were battling each other in pop locking, and the rest of the crowd was just standing around or sitting down on the edge of the stage. Mar Mar was drunk and was having the time of his life.

Snub stumbled over to the DJ booth and started giving out shot outs. "I wanna give a shot out to my little brother, Mar Mar. Welcome home, bruh! To the big bruh Shice, my niggas BG, Will, Menace, Mally G, to the whole High and Spruce, Astor Street, to all my Murda homies! Blat! Blat! Oh, one more thing, shot out to the other big bruhs, Na Blood and One Pac, love that nigga!"

Club music was banging through the speakers and the party was getting wild. *"Follow me…Why won't you follow meeee, to a place… Where we can all be freeeeee…"*

A girl was bent over pushing her butt against Mally G's dick while he was leaning back letting Snub hold him up. *Damn this bitch hurting the shit out of my nuts.*

Menace was in the corner dancing with a girl as well. BG and Shice were sitting in the cut watching the whole scenery. BG had the Tec 9 under his jacket hanging from a string. Will was pissy drunk sitting in the corner of the stage nodding off.

A crowd of people packed around Snub on the stage while he B-Walked and threw up gang signs. Mally G was watching in awe while Snub was killing the Blood dance. Another Blood entered the spotlight and started dancing as soon as Snub stopped and stepped back.

"Yo, you gotta teach me that shit!" Mally G yelled into Snub's ear over the loud music.

"That's called the Blood Walk not the neutral walk!" Snub replied before walking off laughing. He lit up a blunt of marijuana and started smoking on the dance floor as if it were legal.

Finisher, Mango, and four other G.K.B. members walked into the club, all wearing black. People felt the negative vibe as Finisher walked through the club with his homies following. Finisher knew the bouncer, and they were able to bring their guns in with no problems.

The club was more packed than usual and therefore it took a while before Mango spotted Mally G. As soon as he saw Mally G's face, he knew he was the one.

"That's him right there!" Mango yelled while pointing at Mally G.

"Stop pointing, you dumb ass nigga!" Finisher barked while giving Mango a cold stare. When Finisher saw who Mango was pointing at, he went into deep thought trying to figure out where he knew Mally G from. After a few minutes it came to him. *Oh, that's the motherfucker I tried to peace before when I came on High Street. He told me he wasn't banging. This should be easy but being as though he 550, let me go holla at Shice first.*

Shice was well respected since back in the days when he started putting in work in Hayes Home Projects. After he got locked up in New York for picking up drugs, he did two years on Riker's Island and became Blood. Finisher had enough respect for Shice to get the green light before he would murder somebody from his block. Bloods stuck together at that time, and therefore Finisher was almost one hundred percent sure Shice would give him the green light after he tell him he killed Str8 Lace. Finisher knew in his heart he had to kill Snub too, but he wanted to investigate first. Everybody that was involved with the death of his cousin had to go, but the triggerman was his only concern tonight.

BG noticed when Mango pointed at Mally G—he'd been watching them since they walked through the entrance. He knew they came in looking for trouble by the way they were moving. Since BG got out of the hospital, he had been extra on-point. Feeling them shells made him realize the streets is not a game.

"Menace!" BG yelled before waving him over.

"BG what's good?"

"One of Finisher's homies just pointed at Mally G. I think they up to some bullshit. Go tell Mally G and the rest of the homies to be 050 and go wake Will fat ass up. He over there in the corner," BG said before Menace walked off.

Moments later Finisher and his crew were heading straight towards Shice and BG.

"Shice, what's poppin, homie!" Finisher said while extending his arm out to peace him.

"I'm bick backing. What's good, Finisher?" Shice replied while peacing him.

"I gotta holla at you about some real shit. Let's walk over there by the bathroom cause this music loud as hell in this bitch," Finisher said while pointing towards the bathroom.

"What you gotta talk to me about? Money, bitches, what?" Shice asked as he began walking towards the bathroom.

"I know who killed Str8 Lace and he in here right now."

Shice was caught off guard by what Finisher had just said, and Shice reaction wasn't the one Finisher was looking for. He expected Shice to be furious and anxious to find out who did it, but his reaction was calm and nonchalant. After seeing Shice's body language, he knew Shice was involved some type of way in his cousin's death. Finisher still played it cool and went by the bathroom to negotiate with Shice as if he wasn't a suspect himself.

"Who you think killed Str8 Lace?" Shice asked while looking directly into Finisher's eyes.

Snub, Mally G, Menace, BG, and Will were all posted up not too far from where Shice and Finisher were conversing. They all were on point, ready for the worst. Mango and Finisher homies were posted up as well.

Finisher frowned and lost his cool. "Who I think killed him! I said I know, not think! That lil nigga right there!" Finisher barked while pointing directly at Mally G.

"Why the fuck you pointing at me!" Mally G yelled while approaching Finisher reaching for his gun.

One of Finisher's homies drew his gun while approaching Mally G causing a chain reaction. Moments later, all of Finisher's and Shice's homies were all aiming guns at each other.

★★★★★

Back in Philly a few hours prior:

ZaZa was calling all her friends one by one trying to find a ride to the party. After four of her friends gave her excuses to why they couldn't go she was just about to give up when her friend Jazmine came to mind. *Oh! Let me call Jazmine I know her dingy ass try'na get out the house,* she thought while dialing Jazmine's number.

"Hello?" Jazmine yelled into the receiver after the first ring.

"Day'um! Why you yelling in my ear, girl? This ZaZa. What you doing?"

"Shit, I'm beat as hell in here. What you doing?"

"I'm try'na go to this party in Jersey, one of my boo friends having a welcome home party. He just got out of jail."

"ZaZa, you know damn well if I go to a party I'm drinking. Who suppose to drive back to Philly after I get pissy drunk?"

"We gone stay at a hotel and drive back in the morning, my treat," ZaZa replied.

"Now we talking! As much as you talk about Mally G, I was ready to meet him anyway! Does he have any cute friends?" Jazmine asked while smiling into the phone.

"Yeah girl, if you can't find no dick at that party then you ain't meant to be a hoe," ZaZa said jokingly before they both started laughing.

"I'm about to get dressed, girl. I'ma call you when I'm on my way."

"Aight, Jazmine. Don't take a million years either. My boo probably at that party dancing with one of them loose ones!"

"Aight, girl. Bye," Jazmine said before she hung up.

An hour later, Jazmine pulled up at ZaZa's house. It was just getting dark out as they got on the highway and were headed towards Jersey.

ZaZa made sure she put on her best outfit. She wanted to look stunning for Mally G. She had on her favorite tight jeans that made her butt appear fatter than it really was. They were cheap and made out of a thin fabric with no back pockets. She had on a red and white DKNY belly shirt that showed off her flat stomach and some red and white Jordan's. She had her hair done in a fresh doobie. She had on her X&O gold chain, matching bracelet, and big hooped gold earrings. She couldn't forget her Cool Water perfume that Mally G loved so much.

She couldn't wait to see him. She dialed his number as they got closer. To her dismay, he didn't answer. *Maybe the music too loud and he don't hear his phone ringing.*

"Damn, girl. What, the party over already?" Jazmine stated after noticing everybody leaving as they pulled up.

★★★★★

Meanwhile, in the club:

"So this what you want?" Shice asked Finisher with an aggressive tone jerking his gun in the air.

Everybody in the party started stampeding towards the exit at the sight of so many guns. There were sounds of girls screaming and shoes stomping the ground as the club cleared out.

"All I want is revenge on the person who killed my cousin, but if this is what you want you know I live for this shit!" Finisher stated, matching Shice's cold stare.

"Look, Finisher! I ain't really with that set tripping shit, but I can't let you do nothing to him," Shice said nodding his head towards Mally G.

"That lil motherfucker killed my cousin! He killed ya homie! What you mean you can't let nothing happen to him?" Finisher barked back in a rage.

"I said what I said. You know I hate talking so take it how you wanna take it! Ya cousin violated so he got what was coming to him," Shice barked back while staring in Finisher's eyes.

"Oh so you gone cross Blood for a 550?" Finisher said before he chuckled. "Aight, Shice. I'ma give you what you want! Be safe, Blood!" He said sarcastically before walking off as all his homies followed behind.

Shice knew he was in their neighborhood, so he told Mally G and them to hurry up and get to their cars. Immediately everybody started heading for the door.

Mally G was walking towards Snub's car when he heard a familiar girl's voice calling his name. When he turned his head, he saw ZaZa exiting a white Ford Probe. She slowly got out of the car, showing off her outfit and slammed the car door behind her.

"Hey, baby!" ZaZa yelled as she ran towards him with her arms open ready to hug him.

Finisher was in a black Ford Expedition with tinted windows parked in front of the club. *There he go, time to finish him,* he thought when he spotted Mally G through the crowd of people.

He rolled down the window and pointed his 44 Bulldog at Mally G's chest. Once Mally G saw ZaZa, his attention was on her and he didn't see the gun sticking out of the window of the truck. Three loud shots rang off. **POW! POW! POW!!!** The shots sounded like someone lit three M80's. Blood splattered everywhere as the limp body fell to the ground.

The Expedition's tires screeched as it pulled off fast leaving tire marks on the concrete. BG pulled the trigger on the Tec as multiple bullets rang out of the barrel. The back window of the Expedition shattered before it disappeared from his sight.

Snub and the rest of their homies left right before the police came. The police put up yellow crime scene tape and blocked off the street. The ambulance came and covered the body and left just as fast as they had arrived. The homicide detectives asked questions as they waited for the coroners to come and pick up the body.

Witnesses said they heard shots then saw a black Ford Expedition pulling off. But the question people really wanted to know was: is this the beginning of a war or was it really finished?

Chapter 8: Born Again

Later on that night:

"Call all the homies. Tell 'em it's an emergency beven. Tell them to come to the jungle ASAP!" Shice said to Snub, Menace, and BG.

They started calling every S.M.M. member they knew to let them know it was an emergency meeting. Before they knew it, the townhouses on Quitman Street was filled with gang members. Nosey neighbors peeked out of their windows trying to figure out what was going on.

Shice was known for getting money, but everybody knew when it came to war, he was a professional at it. He was unpredictable. Once he ordered his little homies to pull up on a block and open fire. He told them to stop at their building and wait once they were done. One of them tried to explain that their enemies would run in the building as soon as their car turned the corner. Shice told him to shut the fuck up and follow orders. When they turned the corner, their enemies ran just as he said they will, but Shice was waiting in the hall and killed every last one of them as they ran in.

"Peace Blood!" Shice yelled while stepping in the middle of about thirty Blood members formed in a circle.

"Peace almighty!" everyone replied.

"I called ya'll here cause we got a lil situation. We about to go to war with—"

A short brownskin guy from Astor Street named Kay cut off Shice, "My fault for interrupting you, big bruh, but we got somebody that's in this circle that ain't family. How that work?"

"Trillz Blood! Pardon us!" another dude said observing the intruder.

Mally G went in deep thought. The vision of ZaZa running towards him with a huge smile crossed his mind before the terrible sound of three shots going off erasing it. Mally G knew if she wouldn't have run up trying to hug him those bullets would've hit him. *I done lost my girl over this shit. Everybody already think I'm Blood anyway. Damn! Shice crossed his own homies for me. ZaZa, I'ma avenge your death!!! I promise.*

"Fuck that! I'm ready to bome home," Mally G said after snapping back into reality.

"This gone be my first time doing this cause, to tell you the truth, you put in more work than most of the niggas in this circle. Mally G, you don't have to get jumped in, you been official in my eyes. Now who disagree with this decision?" Shice asked before looking around the circle. Nobody said a word as everyone looked around at each other for a response.

"I disagree with that shit!" Everybody looked confused as Mally G continued. "All ya'll nigga's got jumped in. I wouldn't even feel official if I ain't get the same. Let's get this shit over with so we could get back to business," Mally G said before walking into the center of their circle with clenched fist.

He had a lot of anger built up and to him this was just a chance to release some of it. Everybody's face turned into Finisher's face as he got ready to fight. Everybody rushed him at once after Shice gave the signal.

"Blat!" Mally G started frantically throwing vigorous punches at everybody in his sight while Shice began to count. "1 Blood, 2 Blood, 3 Blood…"

He went at the guy in front of him and knocked him on his back pockets. Punches were hitting him from all angles. One caught him hard in the mouth, busting his top lip.

"17 Blood, 18 Blood…"

He was getting dizzy after 18 seconds, but the sight of Finisher in his mind kept him on his feet. His body became numb as he was swinging wild hard blows striking everyone in his perimeter. He was getting hit with multiple blows to the face but kept swinging as if he hadn't felt them. Being as though there was so many people, it actually worked out in his favor because they were so bunched up and crowded that it was hard for anybody to get a clear open shot.

"30 blood, 31 blood. Blat!! Blat!!" Shice yelled, causing everybody to stop swinging.

Mally G put his hands on his knees and hunched over while breathing heavily. He had a busted lip, a knot on his forehead, and a minor scrape under his right eye.

Shice approached him, peaced him, and then handed him a red bandana. "Welcome home, bruh! You a part of the family now, lil bruh. Wear that with pride!" Shice said before giving him a hug. "You good?" he asked after stepping back and analyzing him.

"Why wouldn't I be? I'm tired as hell, though. I gotta stop smoking so much bali," Mally G answered still trying to regain his breath.

Everyone else walked over and peaced Mally G one by one.

"Damn scoob, you kicked up. I ain't think you had that in you," Snub said in between laughs before peacing him.

"We finally got ya ass," Menace said with a huge smile on his face.

"Aight! Let's get back to business!" Shice yelled before everybody formed back into a circle while getting quiet. "Aight, now look. We about to go to war with Finisher from Elizabeth Avenue."

"What's the beef over?" somebody in the circle asked.

"Str8 Lace had to go cause we found out he robbed Will and shot BG. We been heard it was him, then I found that gold plated 44 that BG got robbed for in his car. That's Finisher's cousin so he try'na revenge Str8 Lace's death. He came to Mar Mar's party on some bullshit! Not only did he disrespect me, he disrespected our entire set. He shot at us, and Mally G lost his girl in the process. B.L. he gotta go!

"The problem ain't with G.K.B., it's with Finisher. The forty-second law in the *48 Laws of Power* is, 'Strike the shepherd and the sheep will scatter.' I say chop off the head and the body gone fall. Finisher is the head. He the shepherd. Once we get rid of him, the rest of them niggas gone fall back. Everybody gotta stay 050.

Ya'll know Finisher play that murda game. Who all don't have a gun?"

Shice stepped back to see who didn't have a piece on them. Almost half of the circle raised their hands. Shice shook his head in disbelief.

"Who all got gun connects?" he uttered. About six hands went up. "Keep ya'll hands up! Whoever don't own a gun better remember who got the connects, cause by next week if ya'll ain't got a gun ya'll gotta answer to me. We Murda. We gun boys! Everybody better have a fucking gun!" Shice yelled with aggression, letting everybody know he meant business.

"Who know Finisher personally?" Shice added, getting back to their main focus.

"I don't really know him that good, but I know where his mother live. She live at 142 Shepherd Ave, off of Bergen Street. My aunt live next door to them. I always be seeing him going there," a short skinny guy with dreads said.

"I don't know him that good either, but I know he be driving a black Expo or a red 300 Lex coupe. One of my bitches live on Elizabeth Avenue," another guy added.

"Who here don't know what he look like?"

★★★★★

Back on Elizabeth Avenue:

"I called ya'll here cause I got a fucking issue! It's a couple of niggas that gotta get finished! Them niggas from High Street crossed the line! I got a stolen Jeep parked by Weequahic Park. Who the fuck ready to put in some work?" Finisher asked his soldiers.

Every person that attended his meeting had their hands in the air. "That's what the fuck I'm talking about. You, you, and you going in the Sport, Mango driving. Me and GK gone do a follow up in the Lex coupe, and everybody else just be on standby."

"Big bruh, fall back. Let me ride. You put in enough work for the hood," a little light skin guy named Jeff said.

"Fall back! Who the fuck you think you talking to! My name Finisher because I finish shit! I don't fall back! Matter of fact, get in the middle of the circle. You, you, and you whoop his ass for saying that stupid shit! Anybody else got something to say?" Finisher barked with sweat dripping down his face as he looked around the circle. Finisher wasn't about talking. He was about doing and wanted to make sure everyone understood that.

*****

Back on High Street:

"For all ya'll that don't know what Finisher look like, I'ma go on N.J.D.O.C. and print out his release picture. We gone get rid of this motherfucker soon. I'm about money, and you can't hustle and beef. Whoever catch that nigga slipping first, I got something for ya'll nigga's. Just make sure ya'll stay on point though cause—"

Shice words were cut short by the sound of Mally G's gun firing at a black Cherokee Sport that came through the alleyway located on the side of the townhouses. Mally G saw the Jeep creeping out of his peripheral vision while everybody else was too focused on what Shice was saying. After he shot at the Jeep, they started shooting back immediately. Everybody started scattering like roaches as a parade of bullets flew through the air. All Shice's homies that had guns on them took cover while pulling them out.

"Them motherfuckers better not make it out that alley! Cut the other side off!" Shice yelled while drawing his gun himself.

The alleyway only had two entrances, the one the Jeep entered on Quitman Street and one on Muhammad Ali Avenue. Mally G, Menace, Mar Mar, and another one of their homies cut the exit on Muhammad Ali Avenue off, leaving Mango with two options: either get past them or back out in reverse.

The guys in the Jeep realized they were cornered off.

"Yo, what the fuck we gone do?" the guy in the back seat yelled frightened for his life. They had no idea that they were going to run into so many of them, so they weren't prepared at all.

"Everybody just get down!" Mango yelled before putting his head down and pressing the gas pedal to the floor.

"Hit that shit!!! Hit that shit!!!" Shice yelled as his homies opened fire on the Jeep.

Hopewell Church sat at the end of the alley and a car could only turn right towards High Street or left towards Quitman Street. The Jeep kept going straight and crashed into the church.

When they were finished discharging their weapons, the Jeep looked like a block of Swiss cheese. Mally G shot ten times, and he still had seven shots left in his seventeen shot P89. He walked up to the Jeep cautiously and saw that they were all dead.

"Yo, what the fuck Mally G doing?" BG asked Shice after seeing Mally G climb into the Jeep. Moments later he returned with three handguns.

"Whoever don't got a gun better come get one!" Mally G said while walking towards Shice and the rest of his homies with a smile on his face. For a brief moment he forgot about ZaZa and felt powerful. A few of them ran towards him and he handed them the guns. Everybody started leaving in all directions as they heard the police sirens from afar.

Shice, Snub, BG and Mally G got into Snub's car and drove off. Menace and the other guys from Astor Street walked down the hill. Mar Mar and Will walked up Quitman Street towards Spruce Street.

"Ay, Will. You seen how I Swiss cheesed that shit!" Mar Mar bragged.

"Yeah, man! That shit was crazy as hell. I thought I was about to get shot. Ya lil ass crazy! After doing all that time, you out here carrying guns already," Will said while putting his hand on his chest checking his heart rate.

Mar Mar laughed, and then said, "Nah my brother must have had two guns on him cause he handed me one once they started shooting."

They were halfway up the block when Will yelled, "Oh shit!" before ducking behind a parked car.

By the time Mar Mar looked to see what Will was frightened by, it was too late. Finisher was squeezing the trigger of his 44 Bulldog aimed directly at his chest. Four shots rang off with every bullet penetrating through his chest. Blood squirted everywhere as the impact knocked him off his feet. Will was terrified by the sight of Mar Mar's stiff body lying only a few feet away from him with blood pouring from his stomach area. The sound of an engine revving as the car pulled off made Will's fear for his life gradually disappear knowing they were gone.

"Mar Mar! Mar Mar!" Will screamed in between sobbing. It was too late. Mar Mar was already dead.

Moments later police cars arrived at the scene. Will had Mar Mar in his arms crying hysterically when they arrived.

"What happened?" Detective Reddick asked as he approached them.

Will was crying so hard Reddick couldn't understand a word he was saying.

"Sir, calm down. I'm going to need you to come down to the station and give a statement of what you witnessed. Do you have identification in your possession?" Reddick's partner Detective Puller asked.

Will didn't say a word. He just shook his head side to side and kept crying.

Chapter 9: War

The next day:

Mally G knew there was a war at stake and standing on the block selling drugs during the day wasn't an option. Besides, he had so much on his mind he couldn't sleep if he wanted to. He lost a close friend and the only girl he trusted in one night. He was laying on his bed thinking about how his life had become so erratic in such a short period of time.

Then his best friend Jay crossed his mind. Just the vision of Jay's face in his mind made him feel fake inside. He felt like he crossed Jay by turning Blood being as though his best friend was Crip. He never had intentions on joining a gang in the first place. He just got caught up in the moment of wanting to get revenge. Seeing ZaZa getting murdered clouded his mind, causing him to make irrational decisions. He would have never joined a gang if he were in his right state of mind. He always lived by his own rules and never wanted to get involved in the gang lifestyle. At the moment, all he wanted was revenge on the person that killed ZaZa and was willing to go through any obstacles to get it done.

At the end of the day, he knew what was done was done and that he couldn't change the past. He looked at the radio clock on his wardrobe, and it read 6:01 am. He decided to go on the block and make some early morning money, assuming his enemies were still asleep. He felt it would be safer to hustle early in the morning because it was easier to watch his surroundings with less traffic around.

When Mally G was walking up High Street towards Spruce Street, he noticed somebody sitting on a black plastic crate in front of the grocery store on the corner, which was closed. When he got closer, he realized it was Snub and he looked real depressed. Mally G could tell from the bags under his eyes that he was either crying or he hadn't gotten any sleep.

"Snub, you aight?" Mally G asked with a concerned expression while walking towards him.

"They killed my lil brother," Snub said in a low tone before lowering his head and shaking it side to side with glossy eyes.

They sat in silence for a moment because Mally G really didn't know what to say. He knew how Snub felt about Mar Mar, and he knew it was nothing to say to bring him back. He couldn't imagine how he would have felt if something happened to his little brother, Amod. They were just celebrating for the return of Mar Mar, and now he was gone forever.

"Look, Snub, stressing ain't gone bring Mar Mar back. I'm fucked up just like you. I lost Mar Mar and ZaZa, but I know if I stress myself out it's just gonna make shit worse. My life will never be the same. The only thing that'll make me feel better is seeing Finisher dead. We gone get—"

His words were cut short by a lady. "Do you got cookies?"

"Yeah, I got dimes how may you want?" Mally G asked.

"Can I have one for eight?"

"Yeah, here," Mally G said after he got a dime out of his pocket and extended his hand out to hand it to her.

"Hold on, nephew. Let me find my money," she said while looking through her pocketbook. Then she dumped all her personal contents onto the ground and sat Indian style while scouring through it.

"Why the fuck you ain't have ya money ready already!" Mally G barked getting impatient. She stood up and started searching her body after not finding it in her pocketbook.

"Oh, here it go!" she handed him a crumbled up ten dollar bill.

"What!" Mally G said after noticing she didn't leave.

"I thought you said you were gone give it to me for eight."

"How you gone come with straight money and expect to get a short!"

"I gotta get some loosies and a stem. Come on, baby," she pleaded.

"Here!" He gave her two dollars back, and she walked off.

Mally G had been saving every dollar that he made. He had plans to step his hustle up and start selling weight. He could have been bought a car, but he had big plans set for the future. After serving that addict and the fact that it was too risky to hustle with the beef and watching out for the police, he knew he had to step his hustle up soon.

Snub pulled out a pint of Bacardi 151 and took a sip. His face twisted up in disgust before letting out a light cough.

"Damn! It's like six thirty in the morning. You wilding, drinking that one-fuck-it straight."

"I'm going through it right now. My lil brother really gone. It's my fault he dead. If he wasn't following my footsteps, he wouldn't have been involved in none of this bullshit."

"Come on, Snub. You know that wasn't your fault!"

After Mally G made that statement, it was replaying in his mind and hit home. He felt the same way. He felt like ZaZa and Mar Mar death was his fault. The image of ZaZa's face after she got shot flashed in his mind. He tried to convince himself that it wasn't his fault by repeating *it's not my fault, its Finisher's fault* in his mind, but it didn't work. He still felt deep down in his heart that it was all his fault. *If I wouldn't of never killed Str8 Lace none of this wouldn't of happened. It wasn't supposed to happen like this.*

Mally G's thoughts were eating him up, so he reached for the liquor and after a few sips he was buzzed.

"Yo, I'm finished my drugs. I'm not try'na be standing out here for nothing," Mally G said, showing Snub the empty bag his drugs were in.

"What you try'na do? It's like 7 o'clock," Snub said.

"Let's go get ya car tinted so we can stake out at Finisher's mother house. I'll pay for the tints," Mally G said as he counted his money.

"Here, you driving. My mind ain't here right now," Snub said before tossing him his keys and taking another sip of liquor.

After they came from getting the windows tinted on Snub's Ford Taurus, no one couldn't even see a shadow from the outside of the car. As soon as they were done, they were on their way to Finisher's mother house when Menace called Mally G's phone.

"Menace, what's poppin, bruh?" Mally G exclaimed.

"Shit, I'm in the hood beat as hell. Where ya'll at?"

"Me and Snub leaving from that lil shop in North Newark. We had to make the g-ride Keizer."

"Tell that nigga to come on Astor and scoop me."

"I'm driving. I'm on my way right now. I'ma hit you when I'm turning down Astor."

"Trillz!" Menace said before hanging up.

"Yo, I'm bout to shoot to the hood and pick up Menace."

"Nah man, fuck that nigga! Go to Finisher's mother house so we can get this shit done. Another nigga is just another witness. Me and you good. Finisher killed your girl and my brother, let's go handle this nigga!" Snub said as his words slurred.

Mally G knew he was drunk and exhausted. He didn't want to take the risk of Snub messing up their opportunity being as though he wasn't in his right state of mind.

"I'm bout to go get him just in case Finisher got niggas with him. Menace a rider. We might need him. You acting like he not our homie," Mally G said, heading towards Astor Street anyway.

"We never fucked with niggas from Astor until niggas turned Blood. Fuck that nigga!"

Mally G knew Snub was only talking like that because of the liquor. He ignored him and kept driving towards Astor Street. When he turned down Astor, he saw Menace standing on a porch from a distance. When they pulled up, Menace approached the vehicle and got in.

"Snub, you aight, bruh?" Menace asked after seeing Snub looking delirious. Snub ignored him and kept looking forward.

"Never mind him he drunk as hell, and he been up all night drinking. He really fucked up over his lil brother," Mally G responded for him.

"I feel his pain, but what's good? We on our way to stake out at Finisher's moms house or what? You already know Shice said to get this shit over with fast so we could get back to this money. Plus, I want that nigga anyway. Mar Mar was a real nigga," Menace said while drawing his 357 revolver and placing it on his lap.

"That's why I fuck with you. We was already on our way there," Mally G replied.

Mally G drove straight to Finisher's mother house. There was a parking spot open a couple feet from the house. Mally G paralleled parked into the parking spot, backing up as close as he could to the car behind him and leaving the wheels facing towards the street just in case he had to pull out fast.

*****

Finisher and GK were in one of Finisher's drug houses on 515 Elizabeth Avenue bagging up dime bags of marijuana.

"GK, what time is it?" Finisher asked while stuffing weed into a small plastic bag.

"It's 1:16," GK said after looking at the time on his phone.

"Damn, I still can't believe they killed Mango, Sy, Mills, and Mike. That's too many niggas gone at one time," GK said still thinking about what happened last night.

"We gone get all them niggas. You know they gonna all go to that lil nigga funeral that I finished last night. I'ma make them respect my name!" Finisher said. "When we—"

"Hold on," Finisher said cutting him off as he answered his phone.

"Big bruh, where you at?" Finisher's little brother, Tony, said into the receiver.

"I'm in the hood, why?"

"It's like 1:30. Daddy coming to get me at 2 o'clock to take me downtown to buy that game. I thought you was gonna bring me the money."

"I'm on my way right now. Calm ya lil ass down."

"Aight, big bruh, thanks. I'ma see you when you get here," Tony said before hanging up the phone.

"Who was that?" GK asked.

"Damn, you sound like one of my bitches questioning who calling my phone!" Finishers barked while frowning.

"Fuck you then. You the one acting like a bitch, getting emotional over everything."

"GK, you ain't gone be happy until I beat that ass! But look, put the bali up and run with me to my mother's house," Finisher replied as he grabbed the last few bags of marijuana.

GK and Finisher's relationship was more like brothers. They both respected each other. Finisher had a hot temper and almost everybody else respected him out of fear. GK was one of the only ones that would speak his mind if he disagreed with something Finisher said. He was also one of the only ones that had enough guts to talk back to him, and Finisher respected him even more for it.

The stakeout:

"Damn! We been sitting her for like four hours, and nobody still ain't come out that house!" Menace said, getting impatient.

"That's why it's called a stake out. We gotta sit here until one of us turn into steak," Mally G said before they broke out into laughter.

"Look, Snub tough ass sleeping like a little baby," Menace said before sticking his index finger in Snub's ear causing him to lightly moan while turning his head.

"Let that nigga sleep. He been up all night stressing over Mar Mar. He need some sleep. Break that bali up so we can get high," Mally G said as he pulled out a Dutch from the glove compartment.

As soon as Mally G got finished rolling the blunt, he noticed somebody walking out of Finisher's motherhouse. "We got some action," Mally G said while tapping Menace arm then nodding his head towards the house.

"Is that Finisher?" Menace asked while squinting trying to get a better view.

"Nah, that gotta be his brother. He looks just like a younger version of that ugly motherfucker."

"We waited this long. Fuck that, I'm about to do that lil motherfucker! Finisher killed Snub little brother with no problem. I'm about to give him a taste of his own medicine!" Menace said before hc clutched his hand around the handle of his 357 then exited the vehicle.

★★★★★

Finisher was driving on Bergen Street around the corner from his mother's house when he noticed a patrol car tailing him.

"I think these pussies about to try and pull us over. I'm bout to turn up my mother block if they still behind us, I'm taking it."

As soon as he turned up Shepherd Avenue, he heard five loud gunshots. Then he saw somebody running towards a silver Ford Taurus, enter it quickly, and pulled off. Finisher saw his mother running out of the house screaming hysterically from the sight of her youngest son lying on the ground bleeding from multiple gun wounds.

"That's my fucking little brother!!" Finisher yelled after seeing his brother body stretched out in front of his mother's porch with a small puddle of blood around his head area.

Blood rushed to his head as he pressed the gas pedal to the floor trying to catch the guys who murdered his brother. From the way he looked, Finisher knew he had received headshots. Getting him to the hospital was pointless, but catching the killers was everything.

The siren on top of the patrol car came alive moments after the shots rang off. "We're in pursuit of an all red Lexus coupe heading north bound up the hundred block of Shepherd Avenue. Send back up and ambulance fast. Shots were fired!"

By the time the patrol car turned up Shepherd Avenue, Mally G had already pulled off. All they saw and heard were sirens coming from a distance. They automatically assumed the police was coming after them, but they had no idea that Finisher was tailing them.

"I got 'em!" Mally G said, assuring Menace that he was about to get away from the police. "Wake Snub up just in case we gotta bail out on feet," Mally G said while making a quick right turn. Then he made a quick left turn and started heading towards High Street.

*****

"Damn! Which way they went?" Finisher asked GK after turning the corner and not seeing them.

"I don't know. I think they went right," GK said, seeing more cars on the right side of the block. Finisher turned right, drove straight, and then finally realized he'd lost them.

"Damn! Damn! Damn!" he barked as he banged his fist against the steering wheel.

He glanced in his rearview mirror and realized the police were still tailing them. He was already beyond mad, but the fact that the cops were still bothering him instead of worrying about the gunshots only made things worse.

"GK get these motherfuckers from behind us!" he barked while handing him his 44 Bulldog.

*****

The homicide detectives were called to the scene after the EMS responders officially pronounced Tone deceased. Finisher's mother was sitting on her porch with her hands to her face crying hysterically when the detectives approached her.

"Excuse me, ma'am. My name is Detective Reddick, and this is my partner Detective Puller. We're from the robbery homicide unit at 22 Franklin Street, and we have been assigned to this case. May I ask whom I am speaking with?"

"My… My name is Linda Richardson… They… They killed my son. He never hurt anybody. He was only a child!" Linda said in between sobbing before she broke down and started crying hard.

"Ms. Richardson, we're going to find the guys that did this to your son, but we're going to need your help. We believe your son's murder is connected to the murders that occurred yesterday. Why do you think somebody would want to hurt your son?"

"My son wasn't involved in anything. They probably thought he was my oldest son Farod," she said trying to regain her composure.

"Why would anybody want to kill Farod?"

"Farod stay in some stuff down there on Elizabeth Avenue. Anybody could have been after him."

Elizabeth Avenue? Hold up—first a girl got shot on Elizabeth Avenue, then the incident happened on High Street hours later. Now this. Yeah, they have to be related, Reddick thought.

"Can you tell us what you saw?" Reddick asked with his pad in his hand ready to take notes.

"I was in the kitchen washing the dishes when I heard gun shots, so I ran to the window to see where my son was at. When I looked out the window, I saw a guy running to a car, and my baby was on the ground bleeding from the head. They killed my baby!" Linda said in between cries.

"Did you see the guy's face or the car that he got into?"

"I couldn't see his face because he was running towards the car when I made it to the window, but it was a gray car like that green one right there," she said, pointing to a green Ford Taurus parked across the street.

"Could you describe to me what he was wearing and about how tall he could have been? Was he fat? What complexion was he, and how was his hair? We're going to need a full description to find the person responsible for your son's death."

Puller was on the side writing everything that Linda was saying down in a little small notepad as well. Linda gave her description of what the killer looked like as Reddick radioed the make and model of the vehicle that was involved.

* * * * *

After Mally G lost Finisher and the police, he kept speeding and driving reckless as if he was still getting chased. He was heading down Avon Avenue on his way towards High Street when he flew past a patrol car doing 70 in a 25-mph zone. Just as they sped past the patrol car the dispatcher called in reporting the official make and model of the car involved in the homicide.

"Be on the lookout for a gray Ford Taurus involved in a 187, suspects are believed to be armed and dangerous. Proceed with caution."

The patrol car that they flew by quickly responded. "This is officer Bracey patrol car 793. I'm in pursuit of a gray Taurus speeding south bound on the 500 block of Avon Avenue. Send back up immediately!"

Mally G looked in the rearview mirror and saw the patrol car coming from a distance.

"Damn, these motherfuckers back on us."

Menace and Snub remained calm. They knew Mally G was a proficient driver, and he always got them away in situations such as the one they were in. Menace kept looking back as the patrol car got closer and closer.

"Damn, that shit coming!"

"Fall back. I got'em!" Mally G said before dropping the gear into low one then swerving from left to right before making a left turn at a rapid speed.

"Snub, hand me that blunt," Menace said while pointing to the blunt in the ashtray as he pulled a lighter out of his pocket. Once Menace was halfway through the blunt, he realized he wasn't a bit high. The multiple police cars so close behind them kept him paranoid and tensed.

"Shit getting hectic. I don't think I could dick off in this slow ass car. We probably have to make it to the hood and jump out," Mally G said after looking in the rearview mirror seeing them gaining speed on him.

They were on South Orange Avenue by Bradley Courts, and High Street was a little distance away.

"Fuck that! I'm bout to shoot at them pigs. That a slow 'em down!" Menace said while gripping his 357 revolver.

* * * * *

Finisher was getting frustrated because the police car was still behind them. Seeing the lights flashing in the mirrors and back window made his adrenaline rush as he tried to plan their next move. At this point, he knew he was out of options.

"GK, if I get locked up, you finished! Shoot at them motherfuckers! Niggas just killed my lil brother, and you try'na go to jail!" Finisher barked while giving GK a cold stare.

GK really didn't want to shoot at the police, but Finisher put him between a difficult spot. GK aimed the 44 Bulldog at the driver of the police car and fired three shots. The back window shattered as the three bullets went through it, hitting the driver directly in the chest.

"You stupid motherfucker! Why you ain't stick your hand out the window?" Finisher exclaimed with rage.

The police car swerved to the right before crashing into a parked car. The officer in the passenger seat was hurt, but still conscious.

He picked up the radio and yelled, "shots fired! Officer down in the vicinity of South Orange Avenue and Columbia. Please send emergency medical services immediately. Officer is suffering from three gunshot wounds to the chest. Suspects fled in a red 300 Lexus coupe with a busted back window heading south bound down South Orange Avenue."

After the dispatch was sent out, every police car in the area was desperate to arrest or kill the people involved. Cop cars swarmed every block in search of the red Lexus with the busted back window. Before Finisher knew it, what seemed to be every police car in Newark was chasing him. GK panicked and tossed Finisher's gun out of the window.

"What the fuck you do that for, you scary little bitch?"

"Fuck you, Finisher! I'm tired of ya shit!"

"Oh you tired of my shit huh! I'ma fin—" Finisher words were cut short by the impact of the airbag crashing into his face.

A SUV cut them off as they ran a red light doing 80 mph. The passenger's side airbag didn't come out, so the impact sent GK flying straight through the front windshield, breaking his neck killing him before he hit the ground. Finisher's head jerked back from the impact of the airbag hitting his face, and it took him a few seconds to realize what had happened. Finisher suffered severe injuries but was lucky to be alive.

The war was finally over, or was it?

Later on that night:

Mally G, Shice, Snub, Will, BG, Menace, and four other guys were standing on High and Spruce conversing outside the liquor store. BG looked around the street before stepping in trying to get details of what happened earlier.

"Damn, Mally G. What happened? I heard ya'll put that work in and got into a hectic chase," BG said in a low tone coming off a bit pushy.

"Shit definitely was a close one. I'm just happy we got away, that's all," Mally G said trying to cut that subject short.

"We was staking out long as hell when that lil nigga walked out the house. I had to get him. You should have seen his face before I shot him. That nigga was scared as hell. Once I got over him and shot him in the head, I knew he was dead. I ain't turn Murda for nothing, I play that murder game for real," Menace bragged while throwing up gang signs.

Mally G was cutting his eyes at Menace while frowning trying to give him the signal to shut up, but Menace wasn't paying attention.

"How ya'll wind up getting chased, though?" one of the other guys named Na Na asked.

"Real talk. Them pussies came out of nowhere. Soon as I got back in the g-ride they were coming. Mal dicked off a.s.a.p. though.

But they jumped back on us on Avon. They was coming so hard they had a gangsta getting nervous. So as I was about to dump on them pussies, they started turning off. I think they read my mind," Menace said before laughing.

"Nah, them motherfuckers turned off cause Finisher shot that cop around the corner from the block ya'll was on. I heard his righthand man GK died when they crashed," Shice said.

"Word! What happened to Finisher," BG asked in excitement.

"They said he fucked up. He gone get smoked for shooting that cop, though. He finished!" Shice said before all of them broke out into laughter.

"Damn, Snub, I'm surprised you ain't get a part of that nigga that came out the house," BG said.

"Man, that nigga was sleeping like a baby!" Menace said while laughing.

"Nigga, fuck you! You bitch ass nigga!" Snub barked while stepping into Menace's face.

"Fuck you, pussy!" Menace barked back while clenching his fist.

"Ya'll niggas better fall the fuck back before both of ya'll be in that circle," Shice threatened as he stepped in between them.

"Yo, that's the cops that was questioning me right there." Will said while following the unmarked police car with his eyes as it drove past.

"That's them big boys. You made it look like regular uniform cops questioned you. What you tell them?"

"Come on, Shice, I told you I ain't say shit. I'm not try'na be food. I know not to snitch."

"I hope you telling the truth," Shice said as he looked Will directly in the eyes. Will cut his eyes away and put his head down.

Damn, why they turn this nigga Blood? He gone be our downfall if shit ever get thick. Fuck it, Snub turned him Blood. I guess he see something in him that I don't, Shice thought.

“I’m about to take it down,” Snub said cutting Shice’s thoughts off before walking away.

“Big bruh, don’t mind Snub. He still fucked up over his brother’s death,” Mally G said after noticing that Snub walked off without peacing them.

“I already be knowing, but he better get his shit together soon if he plan on keeping that status I gave him,” Shice said before he peaced everybody and pulled off in his Nissan 300zx.

Chapter 10: More Money More Problems

Four months later:

Only a few months passed, but so much happened in such a short period of time. Mally G stepped his hustle game up to the max. He was selling grams of cocaine and fifty-dollar clips, and business was looking better than ever. He met a connect through Menace that had pure cocaine at an unbelievable price.

Mally G quickly became one of Shice's favorite lil homies as he had all the qualities Shice looked for in a lil homie. He was thorough, he moved smart, and he wasn't flashy—he was all about his money. Mally G was the youngest Blood that Shice had ever gave high status to and the only Blood that got status in such a short period of time.

Mally G was a senior in high school driving a mint green 325 BMW with peanut butter leather seats and BBS rims. He played broke for so long almost everybody except Menace was surprised when he bought his car. Menace wasn't surprised because he was the one who begged him to buy it in the first place. Mally G believed a car like that would cause too much unwanted attention, but he bought it only because he caught a steal. He looked at the car as a flip because he knew any moment that he could sell the car and make a profit.

Mally G was sitting in the stairwell at school listening to music when a girl walked over to him with a newspaper in her hand.

"Ain't you from High Street?" she asked.

"Yeah, why you ask me that?"

"You know him?" she asked while pointing to a picture in the newspaper. Mally G's heart dropped from the site of Menace's face in black and white staring back at him.

★★★★★

After Snub's little brother Mar Mar was murdered, Snub never fully recovered mentally. He was always a grimy dude with a cold heart, but, after that incident, he really became ruthless.

The beef with G.K.B. had calmed down after Finisher was incarcerated, and therefore Shice told all his homies to let the beef die. But Snub was still emotionally distressed over his brother's death, and he didn't want to listen. He still killed every G.K.B. member he caught slipping, as if that was going to ease the pain. Shice took his status momentarily for disobeying his order, but Shice knew eventually he would give it back once Snub got back focused. Snub was one of the first ones that Shice turned Blood, and he was a loyal thoroughbred.

Mally G fell under Snub when he turned Blood because he was the closest to him, and he had a lot of respect for him. Snub schooled Mally G on a lot of stuff in the streets. He taught him things like how to maneuver around the police and how to stack money. He broke down how the cops manipulate people into snitching on themselves and others.

Mally G trusted Snub with his life and was hurt when he found out Snub got arrested for attempted murder on a G.K.B. member. Before Menace got incarcerated, Mally G and him put some money together to get Snub a good lawyer, but his bail was too high to bail him out and nobody had property to put up for him.

★★★★★

Back at school:

Mally G's heart skipped another beat when he read the headline above Menace's photo: **"Gang Member Charged with Homicide from September's Shooting Spree."**

"Let me see that real fast," Mally G asked as he took the newspaper from the girl's hand and started reading.

> **Justice may be close for one Newark family tonight after a long-awaited arrest. An**

alleged gang member was arrested last night and charged with the murder of Tony Richardson, 14, of Newark N.J.

The mother of the deceased, Linda Richardson, 42, of Newark N.J. identified Tyrone Watson, known as 'Menace', 17, of Newark N.J. as the triggerman. Richardson told reporters that the detectives on the case promised her they would find the person that was accountable for her son's death. She stated that she would never forget the perpetrator's face and as difficult as it was identifying him, she said she's happy someone was finally going to answer for the killing of her son.

Detective Puller reported, "as soon as the incident occurred, me and my partner knew the gang members from High Street were involved. We just had to do a thorough investigation to pinpoint exactly who pulled the trigger. The arrest would have never been possible without tips from our confidential informant. Six people lost their lives in that shooting spree. There are more killers roaming the streets, and this is only the beginning of our investigation. Now that we have a confidential informant cooperating, hopefully our investigation will end with every person involved in this incident behind bars."

Mally G dropped the newspaper and started heading towards the door as one of the security guards called his name. He ignored him and kept walking.

When he entered his car and started the ignition, 2Pac's "When Thug's Cry" was banging through the speakers. *"Motherfuckers die, don't ask why... When thugs cry. We don't shed tears we shed blood, do you still wanna be a thug? When thugs cry..."*

Mally G turned the music all the way down. He needed silence to clear his head and get his thoughts together.

Confidential informant? Damn! Who the fuck snitching? I hope it ain't Will. It's gone hurt me to kill him. Shit! I told Menace about running his mouth. When I find out who it is, I'ma make sure he ain't alive to testify. Maybe it was Na Na or S.O. They were there when he was running his mouth. Damn, it was like ten of us out there who could it be? But the whole hood know Menace did that shit. What the fuck I'm gonna do?

His thoughts were cut short when he saw his little man Sal walking down Astor Street. *I'm about to scare the shit out of his lil ass,* Mally G thought as he pulled up on Sal fast and pressed the breaks… Scrrrrr…

Pow! Pow! Sal reacted instantly and let two bullets go out of his 22-caliber handgun he had in his hoodie.

"Oh, shit! My fault, big bruh. You can't be pulling up on a nigga like that. Shit real out here!" Sal said while tucking his 22 back into the front pocket of his sweater.

"Yo, get in. I need to holla at you," Mally G said waving his hand, signaling for him to come.

"Here, this for your window. I'm happy I missed you," Sal said trying to hand Mally G some money.

"Keep your bread. That was my fault, but check this out. I got a money proposition for you. You heard Menace got bagged for a body, right?"

"Yeah, I just found out from Simba not too long ago."

"Well, look, if you try'na make some real money, bome on High and Spruce at 5 o'clock today. Menace was one of my main dudes down here, so I'ma need somebody to take his place."

"Say no more. I'm there."

"I'm bout to go get my window fixed then go handle some business. I'll see you at five," Mally G said in between laughs before he shook Sal's hand, leaving his index and pinky finger out forming a five-point star.

"Aight" Sal said before he exited the car.

Mally G knew he had to recruit soon since Snub and Menace got locked up and Sal was the perfect candidate. He grew up on High Street and lived two doors down from Mally G. He moved on Astor Street with his aunt and cousin, Simba, after his mother got strung out on heroin. Mally G always looked at Sal as if he was his little brother because he reminded him of himself when he was younger.

Sal shot and killed his own father at the age of thirteen. His father used to abuse him and his mother, and that was the reason his mother got hooked on drugs. When Sal found a gun in an abandoned building near his house, all he could think about was the satisfaction he would get by watching his father suffer and die. In that moment, he knew he was going to murder his father with that gun. After finding the gun, his days were consumed with planning out the kill. One day, when he saw his father going in the same abandoned building to use drugs, he put his plans into action.

After he killed his father, his conscience didn't bother him, nor did he regret it. Even witnessing his father plead for his life before he pulled the trigger didn't phase him. He actually enjoyed it. He knew his father wasn't loyal, and he had zero respect for him.

He never told anyone what he did except his cousin Simba and Mally G, the two people he knew he could trust. Mally G helped him get rid of the dirty gun and told him not to tell anyone if he wanted to get away with it. Sal respected and looked up to Mally G, so he listened and never told another soul a word about it.

Sal sold marijuana and was making a little money, but he knew messing with Mally G meant seeing some real money. He was fourteen years old (only three years younger than Mally G), but he still looked up to him. Mally G always looked after him and made sure he never went to bed hungry when his mother was doing badly. The love they had for each other was deep.

★★★★★

Later on that day:

Mally G turned up Clinton Avenue and was driving up High Street when he saw two of his homies standing in front of building #777.

"Yo! Ya'll know it's almost 5 o'clock. Ya'll better start making it up the hill. Niggas getting D-P'ed for coming late to the meeting without a valid excuse," Mally G yelled.

"Trillz! We on our way right now."

When Mally G pulled up to the light on the corner of High and Spruce, he spotted Sal and Simba standing by the buildings. *That's why I love that lil nigga,* he thought as he paralleled parked.

It was about thirty S.M.M. Blood members standing in front of building #725 when he exited his vehicle. "What's poppin, homeboys!" Mally G said as he approached the crowd and started peacing them one by one.

"Ayo! Everybody go in the back before the pigs run down on us!" Shice yelled before everyone started walking into the building.

"Mally G, what's good, bruh? Ya'll deep as hell!" Sal said, observing all of them walking into the building.

"Yeah, we deep, but everybody ain't real. I need more real niggas on the team like you," Mally G said before smiling.

"Real talk, I wasn't off that gang shit, but I'll fuck with it on the strength of you. I'll ride with you no matter what, so I'm already affiliated. Plus, I know you won't steer me in the wrong direction."

"Trillz, you already know we been family."

"I'ma be under you, right?" Sal asked with a frown letting him know he wasn't trying to have nobody else as his big homie.

"Yeah, you gone fall directly under me. Damn, that's crazy you gone be my first pup."

"That's what it is," Sal said, shaking his head up and down with a huge smile on his face.

"Fuck that. I'm boming home too then!" Simba said in excitement.

Mally G was caught off guard. He just looked at him with a confused expression. He really didn't know Simba that well. He just knew him as Sal's cousin, but he didn't have a clue how tough he was.

"Big bruh, I wouldn't steer you wrong either. My cousin go hard. This my right hand right here. It won't be right if we both don't turn Blood together. We do everything together," Sal said after seeing Mally G's facial expression change.

"Look, I'ma take ya word cause I got hella love for you, but if any of the homies say he not Murda type, I can't help him."

"I'm telling you he good. Anybody that know him a vouch for him."

"Aight, follow me."

They walked in the building through the narrow, dimly lit hallway and then exited through the back doors. Everybody in the back formed in a circle with Shice in the center. Mally G walked in the center next to Shice while Sal and Simba fell in place within the circle.

"Peace Bloods!" Mally G yelled.

"Peace Almighty!" Everybody responded.

"Sal, bome here," Mally G said as he motioned with is hand for him to come.

Shice and Mally G fell into the circle leaving Sal in the center by himself.

"Sal, you ready for this B-life?" Shice asked.

"Nigga, I was born ready. I'm ready for whatever!" Sal spoke with an aggressive tone.

"Why you wanna be Blood?" Shice asked.

"Real talk, first I wasn't off this shit cause I know some of these niggas in this shit be straight pussies, but I know it's some real nigga's too like you, Mally G, Menace, and Snub. I'm from High, so I'm riding with ya'll regardless. I might as well be official."

"Trillz, you got the green light from me. Does anybody else want to ask him anything or disagree with him bumming home?" Shice asked while looking from side to side.

"What you got to offer, Blood?" Na Na asked.

"Na Na, you ain't even built like that! What you got to offer me?" Sal said with even more aggression, while shooting Na Na a cold stare.

"Hold! Hold! Hold! Sal, you brazy as hell." Shice said while laughing.

"Sal, nigga's ain't coming at ya neck. This just regular shit niggas ask when somebody bumming home," Mally G confirmed.

"Oh, aight. I thought he was on some bullshit cause nobody else had shit to say, then he gone talk about what I have to offer. I'm saying I could offer hella shit: my loyalty, my love, I get money, I put in work, niggas know me! I'm offering a real nigga to ya'll team—something that's rare!" Sal said while looking around the crowd.

"Blat!" Shice yelled before he started counting.

After the signal, everybody rushed Sal while throwing punches. Punches were hitting Sal from all directions as he tucked his chin in and started throwing punches back. Simba ran in the crowd and started swinging on the guys that was jumping Sal.

"5 blood. Hold! Hold!" Shice yelled causing everybody to stop.

"Where the fuck this lil nigga come from?" Shice said while pointing at Simba.

"I'm not gone sit here and watch ya'll jump my cousin. You bugging, dawg!" Simba said looking Shice straight in the eyes. Shice started smiling because he admired the young boy's heart.

"He supposed to be boming home next," Mally G said.

"How old is ya'll?" Shice asked.

"We both fourteen. Why?" Sal said while breathing hard.

"Mally G, I like these lil motherfuckers! Both of ya'll get in the middle." Once they were both in the center Shice yelled "blat!!" before he continued counting. "6 blood, 7 blood…"

Everybody rushed both them, this time swinging flurries trying to knock them down. They were back to back swinging hard bolos at everybody around the perimeter.

Sal was catching the worst end of the beat down. He fell on one knee and had to cover his face to push himself off the ground. Once he got back up, it seemed as he had a new tank of gas. He was rushing people and swinging hard as he could. He hated the fact that they got him down and caused him to ball up. It made him feel weak, which caused him to become furious.

“31 Blood. Blat! Blat! Yo, yo!” Shice yelled because Sal kept swinging after the signal was given to stop.

“Nah, that motherfucker hit me after you bust the gun. I’ll fuck him up one on one!” Sal said breathing hard standing in the guy’s face with his hands clenched.

Shice walked over to them, put his hand in between them and said, “Fall back, lil homie, you brazy as hell! I’m calling ya lil ass Brazy Boy from now on.”

Everybody peaced Brazy Boy and Simba before the meeting proceeded.

“Aight, I got a big issue. Everybody know Menace locked up for a body, right?” Mally G said before looking side-to-side while studying everybody’s facial expressions.

He then went in his pocket and pulled out a newspaper. He read the entire article as everybody sat in silence. As soon as he was finished reading, Shice ordered everybody to lift their shirts while him and Mally G checked them for wire taps. Once they searched everyone, he continued.

“I don’t know who snitching right now, but best believe we gone find out who it is. We don’t tolerate that in our family. I hate a snitch more than I hate an official pig. Snitches fucked up the Mob, snitches fucked up the Black Panthers, and snitches even fucked it up for runaway slaves. I’ll be damned if I let it fuck up Sex Money Murda! I can’t wait until I find out which one of ya’ll snitching!” Shice was very aggressive as he looked in everybody’s face and paced around the circle.

“The books is closed. Nobody else joining the family until we back right. We not having no more meetings until this shit come to the light, but dues still getting collected every Sunday so meet up with BG and have ya 31 dollars. I'm ending this early cause I can't say much knowing one of ya'll eat cheese! Peace Blood!"

"Peace Almighty!" Everyone replied before Shice walked out of the center.

Mally G peaced everybody before him, Brazy Boy, and Simba entered his car. He drove on Brunswick Street to his stash house, a two-story town house. Once they were inside, he locked the door and pulled out a kilo of cocaine. He gathered up some baking soda, a scale, a blender, and a visionware Pyrex pot. He cooked the pure cocaine into crack cocaine as he taught them step-by-step.

"This is what me and Menace get rich off. You see how I turned a hundred grams into a buck fifty. I'ma need ya'll to help me bag this shit up. The visionware pots are the only ones you can take straight from the stove to the freezer without it cracking, so don't try that with no other pots.

"Ya'll gonna supply the hood now. Everybody from Astor Street gotta cop off ya'll or answer to me. I'ma let everybody know what it is so ya'll don't have to do much. Money gone come fast. This ain't like weed money. Make sure ya'll stack ya'll money cause this shit don't last forever. All that flashy shit ain't official either. All it do is make motherfuckers hate, the Feds watch, and make you waste money on nothing.

"Don't get me wrong. Don't be tight on yourself. We only live once, but stack ya dough and look for a way out. If you wanna buy a car that's cool, but if you can't buy that same car five times over then you can't afford it. Treat everything you buy like that and that helps you to determine whether you can afford something or not!"

Brazy Boy and Simba sat in silence while Mally G dropped a few jewels on them.

"Ya'll ready to get rich? Well, let's get it!"

Chapter 11: Friend or Foe

Two months later:

A couple days after Mally G turned Brazy Boy and Simba Blood, he was at the Exxon gas station on Clinton and Elizabeth Avenue, when somebody shot at his car. He had no idea who did it, so he kept a gun on him everywhere he went since that day. He ended up getting locked up for a gun but was released to his mother the next day because it was his first juvenile charge.

Other than that, everything had been going great. Brazy Boy and Simba together were unstoppable. They moved more cocaine in one day than Menace used to move in a week. Mally G was seeing more money than ever, and his connect started fronting him kilos and dropped the price down because he moved the product so fast.

Menace and Snub were both still locked up. Menace hadn't gotten his discovery yet, so he still didn't know who was snitching on him. Snub's bail was still too high for them to post bail without property. Everyone else was still doing what they did in the streets—some progressed while others still going in circles, hustling backwards.

Mally G was in the house getting dressed for another day of gang banging. He put on a red long john long sleeve shirt and a short sleeve red Dickie shirt. His shirt was custom made with material from a red bandana sewn on the collar, pocket flaps, and one whole bandana on the back. He had on blue PePe jeans with the red nets on the knees that were visible once they were zipped down. He finished his outfit off with some red Converse Chuck Taylors and a red 49er's fitted cap.

Just as he got finished tying his thick red laces, putting his black and red beads around his neck, and placing his red bandana into his right back pocket, his phone began to ring.

"Shice, what's good, big bruh?"

"Mal, where you at, lil bruh?"

"I'm about to leave out the house. Why, what's poppin?"

"Trillz, hurry up and bome to the hood and make sure you bring that with you."

"Say no more!" Mally G said as he hung the phone up and rushed out the door.

He knew something bad had happened by the way Shice was talking. He walked past his car and walked up the street in deep thought. *Damn, what the fuck done happened now? I hope he found out who snitched on Menace so I can take care of their ass.*

Shice, BG, and Will were standing in front of 91 Spruce Street when he walked up.

"Big bruh, what's poppin? Who gotta go?" Mally G asked before peacing them.

"I don't know, Will and them said a brab walked through here flued up and went on Barclay Street."

"Damn, you had me thinking you found out who told on Menace. Who was the nigga, that lil fake tough nigga Ray Rizzo?"

"Nah, I don't know. I never saw him before. He must of just started hanging on Barclay," Will answered.

"Fuck it. Come on, Will. We bout to walk through they hood," Mally G said before he started walking down Spruce Street heading towards Barclay.

As they were walking, Will kept looking at Mally G strange. Mally G caught his stare and said, "Damn, why you keep looking all scary? You good?"

"Yeah, I was just wondering would you let me hold the ratchet?" Will asked.

"Hell no! I got it," Mally G responded with a frown.

"Come on, Mally G. You put in hella work for the hood. Let me get my name up a lil bit," Will said in a whining tone.

"Aight. Here, don't do no dumb shit!" Mally G said while handing him his P89 Ruger.

As soon as they turned down Barclay Street a little dark-skinned guy with a purple bandana tied on his head rolled up on a push scooter and said, "Ya'll know this a Crip hood, right?"

Mally G remained silent. He wanted to see how Will would handle the situation.

"Yeah, we know that this a Crip hood. We don't mean no disrespect. We just taking a short cut to get to where we going. One of your homies walked through our hood earlier."

"Aight, Cuz, c-eazy," the guy said before riding off on his scooter.

Mally G was furious, he hated when a Crip called him 'Cuz', 'slob', 'salami', or a 'corn.' He knew those names were only used to disrespect a Blood. *Why the fuck did I give this nigga the gun. I would have killed that lil nigga, and he talking bout no disrespect.* Mally G snapped back into reality when he heard a guy at the end of the block yelling out.

"Blat, blat killer!!!" while throwing up Crip gang signs and walking towards them.

A huge smile appeared on Mally G's face as he looked at Will and shook his head up and down letting him know it was time to prove himself.

"That's the nigga that came through our hood," Will said as Mally G saw the fear appear in his eyes.

"Blat, blat killer!" the guy yelled out again getting even closer.

"You ready?" Mally G asked, knowing it was about to be on.

"Yeah, I'm ready!" Will replied sounding confident, putting Mally G at ease.

Mally G's heart dropped when he realized who was walking towards them. They recognized each other around the same time.

"Word up, Mally G, you turned slob on me?" Jay said looking Mally G directly in the eyes.

Mally G was at a loss for words. He felt like he crossed his best friend and had no logical explanation to give.

"And you with this bitch ass nigga!" Jay said as he walked towards Will with clenched fists. Will took two steps back then drew the P89 from his waistline. "I'ma kill you pussy!" Jay said while back peddling.

POW! POW! Will closed his eyes as he pointed the gun towards Jay and fired twice.

"G'z up!" Jay yelled as he ducked behind a car.

Will put his head down while running and shooting behind him blindly.

"G'z up!" Jay yelled as he stood up from behind the car holding his hand in the air formed like a G.

Mally G just stood there in a daze. His body was there but his mind wasn't. By the time he snapped back into reality, Will was already halfway down the block. Mally G took off running and as he ran, he heard a guy yelling, "Get him, Cuz! Get him!" He was hoping nobody started shooting at him because Will ran off with his protection. Mally G caught up with Will fast, being as though Will was fat and slow. They cut through High Park Garden complex and when Will tried to jump the gate on Quitman Street, the bottom of his pants got caught on the top of the gate.

"Mally G, help me!" Will said hanging upside down as Mally G approached him.

"Where my gun at?"

"Right here."

"Give it here!"

Mally G grabbed his gun and ran off, leaving Will still hanging on the gate. He ran to the back of 91 Spruce Street and stashed the gun just in case the cops came through. By the time he came out the back Will was standing next to Shice and BG telling them his version of what occurred.

"Yo! Ya'll heard them shots? I was dumping on that nigga! Guess who the fuck that was? That was that brab nigga, Jay. He lucky he was ducking behind that car or I would of killed his ass."

Shice took notice to the blank look on Mally G's face and ask him if he was all right.

"Yeah, I'ma lil fucked up. Shice, you know me and Jay been best friends as far back as I can remember. I never was a fake nigga in my life, but I feel so fake right now. I'm about to shoot to my house. I'ma holla at ya'll later."

"Hold up, Mally G, let me holla at you," Shice said while approaching him.

"Look, I understand how you feel. I know you and Jay go way back. You know it's against the rules to fuck with brabs, but I'ma give you a pass with Jay. Don't let him sleepwalk you, and remember you **Too Real to Be Fake!** Hit my phone when you bome back outside."

Mally G walked off in silence after he peaced Shice. He was on an emotional roller coaster, and all he wanted to do was lay back down.

*****

Back on Barclay Street:

"Jay, you aight Cuz?" Cracc Loc asked while approaching him.

"Nah, Cuz. I'm fucked up."

"You hit?"

"Nah that pussy ass nigga missed!"

"Then what's wrong?"

"That was Mally G with that nigga that was shooting, my best friend I was asking you about," Jay said lowering his head and shaking it from side to side while taking a deep breath.

"Damn! Jay that's crazy you was just asking me about that nigga. Talking about he'll never cross you, and he'd turn Crip before slob. I guess he ain't see shit ya way. I told you that you can't trust a nigga from a slob hood. What you gone do now?"

Jay stood there silent for a moment. "I don't even know, Cuz. He really crossed me."

"Well, look we got a trey sixty at 6 o'clock. I'm about to push to my crib. I'll see you at the meeting."

"Aight, Eastside!" Jay said before throwing up gang signs.

*****

Mally G was walking up the stairs in his house when his mother called his name.

"Huh, ma," he replied while standing in the entrance of her bedroom.

"I'ma need you to watch your brother tomorrow. I gotta handle some business."

"Aight," he responded in a low tone.

"Boy, what's the matter with you?"

"Nothing," he said in a low tone with his head down.

"Jamal, come here. Sit down and tell me what's wrong with you."

Mally G walked in and sat down next to his mother on the bed as he began his story. "Jason came home."

Amirrah was waiting for him to finish, but he sat there silent. "Jamal, you trying to tell me you over there looking sad because your best friend is out of jail? That don't make any sense!" She was staring at him looking confused.

"Yeah, he Crip and I'm Blood. I don't know what to do."

"Jamal, you can't be serious. Ya'll been like brothers since you were born. Jason is family. You gone put some colors before your family?"

Mally G sat there in silence as his mother's words cut through his heart.

"Jamal, Blood and Crip both was made up by some people you don't even know. You not about to let some made up shit get in between the friendship you and him have. Jason cares about your ass. Them boys you run around with in the streets don't give a fuck about you, boy. All you have is your family, and don't let nothing get in between that. Jamal, believe what I'm saying, don't learn the hard way. Do you have Jason's phone number?"

"No, but I got Karen's number."

"Call Karen and get Jason's number. Ya'll not about to let that stupid gang shit get in between ya'll."

"Aight, ma, I'm about to go call her now."

He walked in his room and got his phone and dialed Karen's number. The phone rung three times, and he was hoping she didn't answer because he didn't know how to approach Jay.

"Who this?"

"This Mally G. You got Jay cell number?"

"Oh, hey Mally! Hold on..." she said before she gave him a number. Then she asked, "Is this your cell phone number you're calling from?"

"Yeah," he answered.

"Aight, I'm about to store it in my phone."

"Aight, Karen."

"Mally G?" Karen yelled, catching him before he hung up.

"Wassup?"

"Could you please do me a favor?"

"Yeah, what's good, lil sis?"

"Could you please not tell him about what happened that day? Jay still looks at me as his little angel."

"I got you. We gone leave that as our little secret, okay."

"Aight. Thanks, Mally. I owe you one."

"Aight, be easy, lil sis," Mally G said before hanging up. As soon as he hung up with Karen he dialed Jay's number.

"Yo!" Jay barked before looking at his phone then putting it back to his ear.

"This Mally G, bruh. I gotta holla at you. I know you feel like I crossed you, and I don't blame you. I just want to explain to you what happened and hopefully you understand. Jay, we brothers and we can't let no gang shit come in between us. I ain't plan for shit to happen like this."

Mally G explained everything that happened: the situation with Str8 Lace making Will rob him, how he killed him, the beef with Finisher, how people was already labeling him as a Blood, and ZaZa and Mar Mar getting killed. He explained to him how he turned Blood without thinking only to get revenge on Finisher. To his surprise, Jay took it better than Mally G expected.

"Mally G, you gone be my brother no matter what, but I can't lie and say I'm not a lil hurt. Damn, Mally G, you really a slob," Jay said before letting out a light chuckle.

"Hold on, bruh. Watch ya mouth," Mally G said in between laughs.

"Mally G, I gotta handle something. I'ma scream at you later, though."

"Trillz—I mean, aight," Mally G said before he hung up.

He felt relieved after talking to Jay. Then some crazy thoughts came to his mind and changed his feelings. *Damn, Jay took that a little too easy. What if he trying to sleepwalk me? I know he's known for that. Shit, I've seen him sleepwalk hella niggas. I know how Jay play. I'ma have to get him first. Damn! But what if I kill him and he really forgave me? Shit! What the fuck I'ma do?*

★★★★★

Jay and about thirty of his Crip homies met up in The Hole on Muhammad Ali Avenue, located across the street from Barclay Street.

They were all formed in a circle when their big homie, Sparky, walked into the center and yelled, "Crips don't die!"

Everybody responded, "We ride and multiply!"

"True, I called this trey sixty for two reasons. The main reason is so everybody could meet the big homie Jay, from Hyatt Court. He gone be on the set because shit hot down the net right now. Pooh Bear and them just got locked up. The pigs try'na get all the big homies in the can. While he on the set, treat him like he me or ya'll know what it is.

"The second reason is, I'm starting to see slobs on Summerset. Ya'll letting them slobs come from High Street and hustle on our set like Crip don't rule. Ya'll motherfuckers better get ya'll shit together!" Sparky said as he looked around at everybody. "Jay, you got anything to say before I end this?"

"Yeah, for all ya'll that don't know I got universal G. Since I been on the set, I seen ya'll nigga's ain't moving left. A slob came through ya'll hood with hella dead on, shot at me, and made it out alive. I'm not gone stress the issue or preach, but ya'll nigga's better stay on ya'll Stacey's cause ya'll ain't on point. Whoever don't got a slammer better get one or be ready for a hardcore. Ya'll could take that as a threat or a warning. Either way, I don't give a fuck! Eastside Cuz!" Jay yelled before stepping out of the center of the circle.

★★★★★

Shice was laying in his bed asleep when the sound of his phone ringing woke him up.

"Hello," Shice said into the receiver.

"You have a collect call from… Menace… If you accept the charges press one."

"Menace, what's good, lil bruh?" Shice said sounding half sleep.

"Damn, big bruh. You sound like ya breath smell like shit. What you just woke up?" Menace asked before laughing.

"Yeah, it's early as hell, but what's good, though? You got some good news for me?"

"Kind of. My lawyer came to see me yesterday. I got paperwork on two niggas. One of them is crazy, though. The name and address is blacked out, so I can't tell who it is. I asked my lawyer if he could find out who it is for me. He said the nigga is their key witness so the pigs ain't try'na give his name up, but he gotta show up in court to testify if I go to trial. That's the only way we gone find out who he is. I think he on the streets still giving them information. That's why they protecting him like that. In the statement he made, he said he was there when I supposedly killed ol boy, and he described everything in detail. The only motherfuckers that were there was Mally G and Snub, and Snub was sleep the whole time."

"So what you try'na say?" Shice asked offended by what he heard.

"I ain't try'na say shit! Mally G like my brother, and deep in my heart I believe he'll never trip nine on me but shit just look funny!"

"Shit do look funny, but I don't think Mally G a go out like that. Who name on the other paperwork?" Shice asked, trying to change the subject.

"The lil nigga, Na Na. He told them he heard me talking about what I did, but he ain't see shit. My lawyer said that's not hearsay because he saying I told him myself. That shit can fuck me up if I go to trial, and he said if anything happen to that lil nigga that they could try and put it on me. Just talk to him and tell him if he don't testify and take his statement back, he not food. Just sleepwalk the nigga until my case is over.

"The description ol boy mother gave the day that shit happened was fucked up too. Other than that confidential informant, shit looking good. Try to put pressure on Na Na to tell you who else snitching. Nine times out of ten they were together because the statements got took the same day."

"You have thirty seconds remaining" the operator interrupted.

"I'ma get at Na Na a.s.a.p. and make everything right. Keep ya head up, we gone get through this."

"Trillz, E.S., big bruh."

"All the time," Shice replied before hanging up.

He laid on his bed and went into deep thought. *Damn, I hope my lil nigga, Mally G, ain't snitching. Nah, it ain't him. Menace was running his mouth to everybody. This shit getting crazy. I don't know who to trust. When did Mally G have a chance to snitch? Oh shit! He did get locked up for a gun and came home the next day. I have to see if that day match up with the day of the statement. Damn!*

Chapter 12: Pain & Pleasure

Two weeks later:

Jay and Mally G didn't let their gang lives get in between their friendship. First, Mally G didn't know if he could trust Jay, but after he took his chances and met up with him, he realized that Jay still had the same love for him as he did in the past.

Ring… Ring… Ring…

"Yo," Mally G said after answering his phone.

"What's cracking, Blood!"

"Jay, you shot the fuck out. What's good with you?"

"Shit, I'm try'na go to that club Brokers in East Orange tonight. It's gone be hella college bitches in there. You try'na go or what?"

"Who suppose to be going with you?" Mally G asked. He didn't want to be around a lot of Crips.

"Me, you, and my whole set," Jay said jokingly before continuing, "Nah, just me and you! I go to the club to get bitches, not hang around a bunch of niggas."

"Aight, I'll go. Just hit me when you ready."

"Say no more," Jay said before hanging up.

*****

BG, Brazy Boy, Simba, and Will were driving downtown in BG's car.

"Yo, stop at that chicken shack so I could get something to eat," Will said.

"Damn! Ya fat ass just ate like two hotdogs, you greedy as hell!" Brazy Boy yelled from the back seat.

"I gotta get some Dutch's anyway," BG said while pulling up in front of the chicken shack on Broad and West Kinney Street.

"BG, ain't that Kay right there?" Will asked while pointing into the chicken shack towards Karen.

"Hell yeah! We bout to have fun with that!" BG said before exiting his vehicle with a huge smile. He approached Karen from behind.

"Kay, what's good ma?"

"Oh, hey BG!"

"What you about to do?"

"I just came from paying a ticket for my brother. I was about to catch the bus home after I get my food."

"You might as well chill with us for a minute. We about to go to my house, chill, and smoke some bali. I'll take you home when you ready to leave."

"I don't know..." Karen said while looking undecided. She continued, "Aight, let me call my brother first because I don't want him to be looking for me. He be acting like he my father sometimes." Karen pulled out her cell phone and dialed Jay's number.

★★★★★

No matter what, Mally G trusted Jay but only to a certain extent. He never trusted anyone one hundred percent. Jay called him and told him to pick him up from Court Street. When he pulled into the housing complex, he had his P89 Ruger laying across his lap. He honked the horn three times before Jay exited one of the town houses.

"Damn! Who you about to kill?" Jay said as he saw the gun when he approached the car.

"You know I don't trust these niggas around here," Mally G said while smiling.

"Ayo, check this crazy shit out!" Jay said excitingly while handing Mally G his phone. Jay had a video of a horse having sex with a human.

"Damn! I'd never fuck that bitch, that'll be like sticking my dick in a hallway. When they come out with this phone? I never saw a phone with videos on it."

"That shit ain't even come out yet. My man got the connect though. I got… Who that?" Jay said cutting his sentence short after hearing his phone ring.

"It say 'my heart,'" Mally G responded.

"Oh that's Karen. Answer it and see what she want."

"Lil sis, what's good?"

"Jay I'm…"

"This ain't Jay. This your other brother, Mally G."

"Oh, hey Mally. What ya'll doing?"

"Shit, we about to go to this club. Why?"

"Nothing. Just tell Jason I said I'm going to Unique's house," Karen lied.

"Aight."

"Mally!" Karen said catching him just as he was about to hang up.

"What's up, sis?"

"You spending the night at our house when ya'll leave the club?"

"No, why you ask that?"

"Cause I wanna see you," Karen said with a flirty tone that caught him off guard. "Mally, you there?"

"Yeah, I'ma tell ya brother you gone be at Unique's house. Bye, Karen," Mally G said, rushing her off the phone before going into deep thoughts. *Damn, lil sis bugging. She getting out of hand. How the fuck could I explain to Jay what happened that night? "Aye, Jay when you was locked up I made a mistake and fucked ya sister." Nah that won't work…*

"What she say?" Jay asked bringing him back to reality.

"Oh, nah. She said tell you she gone be at Unique's house."

"Oh, aight."

* * * * *

BG went to the liquor store and brought a fifth of 151 Bacardi, then they all went to his apartment on Spruce Street. BG, Will, Brazy

Boy, Simba, and Karen were all smoking blunt after blunt laughing on the couch, talking and listening to music. They were sipping on their cups of 151 and Pepsi. Before they knew it, they were all high and intoxicated.

"Kay, come here," BG said as he tapped the couch next to him signaling for her to sit next to him. "Show me some love," he said before he zipped down his zipper and pulled his dick out.

Brazy Boy and Simba was both shocked by BG straight approach. To their surprise, she lowered her head and placed her mouth around his dick. BG looked at Brazy Boy and motioned for him to join in. It didn't take long before Simba, BG, and Brazy Boy were taking turns having sex with Karen. First, BG was getting oral sex while Brazy Boy was sexing her from the back. Then, Brazy Boy was getting oral while Simba was sexing her from behind. They kept rotating until everybody was satisfied.

Will just sat there and watched the entire time. He was embarrassed to get nude in front of his friends and knew they would joke on him about his little dick and sloppy body. He took Kay into the back room once they were finished.

"Call Mally G. I know he want some of our jump bitch. She the prettiest jump I've ever seen," Brazy Boy said after Will and Karen went into the back.

"Hell no! Kay is like a sister to him. Last time we called him, he sent the bitch home. We can't let that happen again!" BG said while laughing.

"Oh, aight. We could call him when we done. Now she got a ride home," Brazy Boy said before they all started laughing.

"Man, turn that music up and pass that Murda juice," Simba said.

Karen walked into the room and sat down on the bed. She was still naked and feeling the liquor. Will removed a 38 special from his waist and placed it on the dresser. Then he removed a stack of money from his pocket and started counting it.

This nigga a fucking clown, Karen thought as she looked at him.

"Kay you know I really like you, right? You pretty as hell. You should be my girl. I don't even care how many niggas you fucked. I'd still wife you. You wouldn't have to fuck nobody else again. I'll make sure you good."

"Nigga, you act like I'm fucking for money. I enjoy fucking, so I fuck!" she snapped, rolling her eyes.

"My fault, baby. I ain't mean to make you mad. I just want you to be my girl."

"First of all, I don't like fat dudes, so me and you a never be. And, second of all, you couldn't satisfy me if I was ya girl."

"Oh, you think I can't satisfy you? Bend over."

Karen chuckled then bent over with her knees and hands on the bed. "Prove me wrong, fat boy!" she said in between laughs.

Will walked behind her and placed his dick into her vagina. He was pumping as hard as he could. He tried to pick up the pace after about two minutes, but his dick kept slipping out of her wet pussy. She chuckled after the fourth time and looked back at him.

Oh you wanna laugh, bitch! he thought as he forced his dick into her asshole. The pain struck her instantly, and it felt like something ripped. He started pumping hard as he could again. A smile appeared on his face when he heard her moan. *Bitch, I told you I could satisfy you, I told you bitch!* he thought while ramming his dick in and out of her ass.

"Stop, stop, please!" she cried, realizing she couldn't take it any longer.

He kept ramming his dick into her ass while holding her down with his weight.

"I thought I couldn't satisfy you! I thought I couldn't satisfy you, bitch!"

"Please, stop! You're hurting me!"

★★★★★

"Yo, you heard that?" Brazy Boy asked BG and Simba.

"Nah, I ain't hear shit," BG replied as he took another sip of his 151.

"I thought I heard somebody screaming. Let me find out Will in there busting her ass."

"Fuck all that. Turn that Pac back up. That's my shit!"

* * * * *

Kay was trying to pull away from Will, but he was just too big. She started kicking frantically and kicked him in his nuts.

SLAP! "You stupid bitch!" Will barked after smacking her to the floor. When she stood up, she saw his gun sitting on the dresser and she quickly grabbed it and pointed it at Will's face.

"You fucking fat bastard! I'ma fucking kill you!" she yelled in between sobbing as blood mixed with spit flew from her mouth.

Pow! Pow! Two shots fired out of the barrel of the gun as Will fell to the floor with tears rolling down his face.

"Get ya fat ass up!" Brazy Boy said while walking past Will. He walked over to where Karen was laying and kicked the gun away from her. Then he pointed his gun at her head.

"Please don't kill me! Please!" she cried.

Damn this like Mally G sister. I can't kill this bitch, Brazy Boy thought to himself.

"Bitch, get the fuck up!" Brazy Boy said when he snapped back into reality.

"I can't, my shoulder!" she cried while placing her hand over the fresh bullet hole in her shoulder.

"What the fuck happened?" BG asked when he entered the room.

"I don't know! I walked in the room and she had a gun pointed at the homie screaming 'I'ma kill you' so I shot that bitch!"

* * * * *

When Mally G and Jay pulled up at the club, the line was all the way down the street. They walked to the front of the line.

Mally G shook the bouncer's hand while handing him a folded hundred-dollar bill. "It's just me and my man right here," he said before the bouncer let them in without giving them a pat down.

Brokers was a huge club with two floors located in East Orange, New Jersey. The first floor was for people twenty-one and older because they served liquor, and upstairs was for people who were sixteen to twenty. That's where the big dance floor was located. It had a small bar that only sold water and juices and a photo section on the far left side next to the restrooms. Mally G and Jay walked straight upstairs to the dance floor.

"Damn, this shit poppin!" Mally G said after seeing how packed the club was.

Jay got behind a woman that was dancing, and she started grinding her ass against his dick as he went with her rhythm. Mally G got behind the woman next to them, and she started dancing then stopped and looked back.

"No, I ain't ugly," Mally G said before she smiled and continued dancing.

They went around the entire club dancing and flirting with every sexy woman before Jay tapped him. "Yo, let's go take some pictures."

When they approached the photo area, there were three women taking pictures.

"Damn! That bitch bad as hell with the pink on!" Mally G said with lust in his eyes.

"Yo, that look like Travis's daughter!" Jay said frowning.

"Who the fuck is Travis?"

"The nigga that killed my brother Darnell."

"Oh, shit! That's India? I had a crush on her since we was little kids. Damn, that is her and she still bad as hell."

"Fuck that bitch! I'ma kill her father soon as he bring his ass home!"

"You right. I'ma fuck that bitch," Mally G said before walking towards her. "Damn, where you been? I was looking for you my entire life," he said while looking her in the eyes.

That punch line was weak, but he cute, India thought. She said, "Yeah, if you were looking for me, then what's my name?" She said smiling as she softly bit her bottom lip, returning his stare.

"Damn, India. You do something special to me."

Her smile quickly disappeared. "For real, how did you know my name?"

"I remembered it cause I had a huge crush on you when we used to live in Hayes Homes back in the day. I was dead serious when I said I was looking for you my entire life. If I was running game, I would have came better than that."

"Damn, that's crazy. I don't know what to say."

"You ain't gotta say nothing. Just put ya number in my phone so I could call you."

"What's your name again?"

"Jamal, but everybody call me Mally G."

"Aight, Mally G. Make sure you use that number."

"Don't worry, I'ma call you every time you leave my sight. Don't go far," Mally G said, laughing before walking away.

When he looked at his phone, he noticed he had eleven missed calls. They were all from Brazy Boy. After they took pictures, he pulled Jay to the side.

"I'm about to go in the bathroom and call my lil bruh back. He called me hella times. Something might be wrong."

"Who? Amod lil ass?" Jay asked.

"Nah, my lil homie Brazy Boy."

"Oh, ya slob brother," Jay said before laughing.

"You got a lot of slob jokes. Brab niggas be funny as hell," Mally G said before they both started laughing.

When they entered the restroom, Jay looked at his phone. "Damn, Karen been blowing my phone up too. What the fuck is this the blow our phone up day," Jay said in between laughs.

Mally G was calling Brazy Boy back while Jay called Karen back. Karen's phone went straight to the answering machine, but Brazy Boy picked up on the first ring.

"Brazy Boy, what's good? Everything aight?"

"Nah, big bruh. Some bullshit happened."

"What you mean some bullshit? Like what?"

"I walked in the room, and Kay had a gun pointed at Will screaming 'I'ma kill you.' I had to shoot her. I ain't kill her though cause BG said she was like ya sister."

Mally G couldn't believe what Brazy Boy just told him, and his heart began pumping extremely fast. His body became hot as his thoughts settled in. "Where she at now? Is she okay?"

"We put her in a cab and sent her to UMD hospital."

"She good?"

"Yeah, she only got hit in the shoulder."

"Only in the shoulder!" Mally G repeated, knowing nothing was good about that. "Aight, I'ma hit you back," Mally G said before he hung up and headed out the rest room.

"Jay, come on we gotta go!"

"What happened? One of ya homies got shot?"

"Nah, Karen got shot. She at UMD," Mally G blurted out still in a daze.

"What? Are you serious? Don't play with me like that Mally G!" Jay said as his heart picked up it's pace.

"Yeah, man. I'm serious. Come on, I won't play about no shit like that."

As they walked to the car, Jay was asking all types of questions. "How did ya lil homie know she got shot? Where was she at when it happened? She good, right? Who shot her?"

"Jay, calm down. She good. I don't know what happened. I'm about to drop you off at the hospital and go find out what happened now. That shit happened in my hood, though. I can tell you that much."

As they pulled up to the hospital, Jay said, "Bruh, make sure you call me and let me know what happened just in case I don't get a chance to talk to Karen. Who ever shot lil sis is good as dead, so hurry up and get back at me."

"I'ma call you as soon as I know what's going on, bruh."

Jay ran into the hospital as Mally G drove off. Jay entered the sterile small hospital room where Karen was located and noticed there were already two detectives interrogating her.

"Oh my God, Jay. I'm so happy you're here!" Karen yelled when he walked into the room just as tears fell down her face.

"Yo, she a minor. Get the fuck out! She can't answer none of ya'll questions until our mother get here!"

"Do you know your little sister was raped before they shot her? We're only trying to help. Do you mind?" Detective Puller asked.

"Yeah, I fucking mind! Get the fuck out, we don't need your help!" Jay barked.

"Okay. We'll be back, tough guy," Puller stated before they left the room.

"Karen, what happened?" Jay said after he closed the door and took a seat next to her.

She started crying harder as soon as they were alone. He sat on the bed and held her in his arms trying not to touch her shoulder and comforted her as she told her story.

"I went on Spruce Street with my friend to see this guy name BG. We were all in the room smoking and then they went into the front and left me in the room with this fat guy named Will. He tried to get me to have sex with him, but I said no. He started hitting me, then he raped me." She started to cry even more.

"Karen, calm down, and tell me what else happened."

"I tried to fight him off me, but he was too big. It was a gun on the dresser, so I struggled away from him after I kicked him in the dick. I grabbed it, but when I was about to shoot him, his friend Brazy Boy came in and shot me first."

"Calm down and stop crying. What did you tell the cops?"

"I ain't tell them nothing. I just told them I got raped and that I was on Spruce Street. Then you came in," Kay said in between sobs.

"Aight, I know all them niggas that did that shit. I don't know how Brazy Boy look, but Mally G said he was his lil homie. Don't worry Karen, I'ma kill all them motherfuckers! If the police question you again say you don't remember nothing after you got knocked out. I can't kill them niggas if they in jail."

Chapter 13: Charge it to the Game

Mally G pulled up on High Street five minutes after he dropped Jay off at the hospital. He was speeding and running lights hastily to find out what happened with Karen. When he pulled up, Will, BG, Simba, Shice, Brazy Boy, and Snub were standing in front of the liquor store. He had to look twice to make sure it really was Snub's face he saw glowing in the dark from the dim liquor store sign light. As mad as he was, a smile still managed to appear on his face from the sight of Snub finally being home. When he approached them, everybody was trying to talk to him at the same time.

"Hold! Hold! Let's go in the back of the buildings!" Everybody followed as Mally G lead them to the back. As soon as they got to the back Mally G began. "Shice, I don't know if you know what's going on, but Brazy Boy shot my sister—Jay's lil sister, Karen. We gotta get to the bottom of this."

"Let me tell my part first being as though I shot her. Right now, I'm looking like the bad guy and it ain't even like that. Me, Simba, and BG was in the front room listening to music. We had already jumped off with her. Will wanted to go dolo. I heard somebody yelling, but I was cooking off that 151 so I just thought it was me bugging. I asked them did they hear something, and they said nah. Then I heard it again, so I went to the back to see was I really bugging. When I walked in, Kay had a gun pointed at Will screaming 'I'ma kill you,' so I shot her. It ain't look like she was playing. I wasn't gone just let her shoot the homie."

"Will, what the fuck you do to make her point a gun at you?" Mally G asked in a stern voice focusing his attention on Will now.

"I was fucking her from the back, then I slipped it in her ass. I guess it was too much for her, so she told me to stop. I tried to put it back in her pussy, and she said she was done. I'm like, 'damn you ain't gone let me get my nut.' She wasn't beat. I was mad as hell, so I started calling her names. We were arguing back and forth, I guess that's when Brazy Boy heard us. Then she spit in my face. I ain't even think, my reaction made me smack her. She fell to the floor, and my gun was in my pants on the floor. She grabbed the gun and pointed it at me, screaming that she was gonna kill me. I closed my eyes. I thought I was shot when I heard the shots ring off until I heard Brazy Boy telling me to get up."

"Fuck that! I told ya'll to leave her alone. Ya'll knew that was like my sister from the first episode. Now look—she in the hospital shot cause ya'll don't listen. BG and Will, ya'll gotta get ya'll ass whooped!" Mally G barked.

"I'ma keep it real, they told me she was like ya sister too. I guess I gotta get my ass whooped too," Brazy Boy admitted.

"I guess I gotta get my ass whooped too," Simba added.

"Mally G, we knew she wasn't your real sister. Whether you like it or not, she's a hoe. I don't know her from a can of paint, and she let me do whatever to her. If I was in your shoes, I'd rather for the homies to have fun with her than our enemies. She a jump. If we don't do her, somebody else will. It ain't no changing her. She like being a hoe!" Brazy Boy said trying to keep it real with Mally G.

"Brazy Boy, you right. I can't hold ya'll on that. Damn, this shit crazy, though. Snub, how the fuck you get out?" Mally G asked switching the subject.

"Remember my man, One Pac, with the white Dodge Viper? He put one of his houses up for me. He put some bread up too so I gotta pay him back. That lawyer you and Menace got me got my bail lowered a lil bit. Good looking, bruh!" Snub said before giving Mally G a handshake and a hug.

★★★★★

Back at the hospital:

I can't believe these niggas really raped and shot my lil sister. Ooooh! I can't wait to watch them niggas die. Them niggas be with Mally G, so it's gone be easy setting them up. Damn, I wonder what's taking that fool so long to call a nigga. Fuck it, I'm about to call him, Jay thought as he walked to the front of the hospital to use his phone.

Ring… Ring…

"Jay, what's good, bruh? I was just about to call you. Is Karen good?"

"Yeah, she living, but its a few niggas that gotta die. You know Karen got raped, right?"

"Nah, niggas ain't say no shit like that."

"Who admits to raping somebody! My sister ain't gone lie to me. The nigga Will raped her. She fought her way away from him and grabbed his gun off the dresser then ya lil bruh, as you call him, shot her. I'ma kill all them niggas! Them niggas raped and shot my sister. It ain't even nothing to talk about. Set them niggas up and nobody a never know you had something to do with it."

"Jay, we gotta get to the bottom of everything first. I don't know who lying. Will's story was totally different. Karen probably made that rape shit up cause she was mad."

"Nigga, you gone take them slobs word over your own lil sister's!" Jay barked with aggression.

"Look, Jay, calm down."

"Calm down! What the fuck you mean 'calm down!' Them niggas raped and shot my sister. Why the fuck should I be calm! You know what, fuck you too then! Don't get hit in the crossfire and tell ya homies to strap up cause it's on!"

Jay slammed his phone shut then opened it back up and dialed another number. Ring… Ring… Ring…

"What's Graping, Cuz?" Sparky said into the receiver after recognizing Jay's number.

"Yo, my lil sister got raped and shot by them slobs on High Street. It's K's up on all of them motherfuckers! They families and everybody gotta go! I know where one of them nigga's mother live at. She gone be dead before the morning. Tell all the homies what it is."

"True, I got you, Cuz. It was time to start eliminating them niggas anyway. I told you they try'na move on Summer Set little by little."

"Start letting the homies know what's cracking. I'm about to go pick up Cracc Loc and head to ol boy's mother house soon as I leave the hospital."

"Aight, G. Safe, Cuz. Eastside!"

★★★★★

Back on High Street:

"Yo, I just got off the phone with Jay, and Karen said you raped her. Don't make me do something to you. Now what the fuck happened?" Mally G yelled while stepping in Will's face.

"Mally G, I swear on B's she lying! I told you what happened, that was the honest truth. You know Kay a straight hoe. She'll fuck anybody. Why would I rape her?"

"Mally G, I believe him. She let us do what we wanted to do to her, and she ain't know me or Simba," Brazy Boy said.

"Mally G, you know how bitches get when they mad. Will ain't rape her. She made that shit up cause she probably ain't wanna tell her brother she was getting jumped. She never mentioned shit about rape before we put her in that cab. She lying," BG added.

"I kind of believe him too, but Jay ain't try'na hear that shit. Call a whoop and tell everybody to stay on point. Jay feels like niggas raped and shot his sister, so he gone go all out. You and Will probably be his main targets so stay 050," Mally G said to Brazy Boy.

"He don't even know who I am, and I ain't worried about that nigga. He a die fucking with me!" Brazy Boy said while adjusting his gun on his hip.

The statement Mally G made had Will's heart doing a hundred miles per second. He knew Jay was a loose cannon. On the other hand, it left Mally G stuck. He couldn't imagine having to take sides when it came to Jay and Brazy Boy. In his heart, he looked at both of them as brothers, but he knew the love him and Jay had for each other was deeper. Knowing Brazy Boy wasn't in the wrong made any decisions harder. One thing for sure was that Jay was coming, and it would be almost impossible to stop that.

*****

"Park right there. We gone walk around there," Jay said as he cocked his 40 cal back. When they approached the door, Jay pulled his red fitted cap low covering his eyes. **Knock! Knock! Knock! Knock!**

"Who is it?" a woman's voice answered.

"It's death!!" Jay responded.

When she opened the door, she found herself looking down the barrel of a gun. Before she could react, a bullet came crashing into her face and many others followed. **Pow! Pow! Pow! Pow! Pow! Pow!**

"Bitch!" Jay said gruffly while wiping blood off his face with the back of his forearm.

*****

Later on that night:

Shice, Mally G, Snub, Will, BG, Na Na, Brazy Boy, Simba, and about five other S.M.M. gang members were standing on High and Spruce when Cracc Loc drove by in a tinted vehicle, observing them as he road by.

Will was going off. "Them niggas gotta die. They killed my fucking mother!" He started crying even harder after making that statement. "How the fuck they find out where I live? Why my mother had to answer the door?" Will said in between sobbing before breaking down and crying hysterically.

Mally G started feeling like everything was his fault again. He knew deep in his heart that Jay would have never knew where Will lived if it wasn't for him taking Jay to his house the night Str8 Lace made Will rob him. *Damn, now Will mother dead. What the fuck I'ma do. Jay getting out of hand.*

"Mally G, let me holla at you real fast," Shice said bringing him back into reality. They walked off to the side.

"Mal, you know I never had a problem with beefing. Shit, I use to live for that shit before I started getting money. But I'm not stupid at all. It's no way we can beef in our situation. I can't even trust these niggas—we got cops in our family. Us beefing with Grape Street Crips only mean dead bodies. We can't afford that especially since we don't know who's snitching yet.

"We can do two things: peace it up somehow, or me, you, Brazy Boy, and Snub can try to take their head niggas out fast—starting with Jay. Ya'll the only niggas I know in my heart that won't snitch. Look at that bitch snitch ass nigga over there like everything cool."

Mally G looked over and saw Brazy Boy, Simba, and Na Na standing there talking. He knew Shice was talking about Na Na.

"Big bruh, I got something in mind. I'ma try to squash that shit. Me and Jay on bad terms right now, but I'ma think of something."

*****

Back on Barclay Street:

"Ay, Jay! I just drove through High Street, them slobs out there deep as hell. The slob nigga you use to fuck with out there too. We could come through both ways Quitman and High Street and finish all them niggas with the choppers. This shit easier than I expected!" Cracc Loc said excitingly.

"Aight, get the g-rides and choppers ready. I'm bout to make a phone call real fast."

Deep down in Jay's heart he couldn't live with killing Mally G. He had love for him that was way beyond gang banging. Mally G had been his best friend since he was a baby. As ruthless as he was, he just couldn't kill him.

*****

Back on High Street:

Just as Mally G was finished talking to Shice, his phone began to ring and to his surprise it was Jay.

"What's good?" Mally G said into the receiver.

"Where you at?" Jay asked.

"In my hood. Why what's up?"

"Bruh, I got hella love for you, and I can't see nothing happening to you. My homie drove through there and saw ya'll out there slipping. Get from out there. Shit might get real in a few minutes."

Oh they thought we were slipping. Only if he knew we got two choppers on each end of the street and everybody strapped. We waiting for something to come through acting stupid.

"Mally G, you there?"

"Yeah, I hear you. We ain't even gotta take it there."

"Mally G, don't start talking stupid again!"

"Nah, I thought about the whole situation. You right. Karen family, so she comes first. I'll help you set up Brazy Boy being as though he the one that shot her."

"I want Will too! Fuck that, he raped her!"

"Jay, I really think Karen lied about that. It hurt me, and I was hoping she had changed so I never told you. I caught niggas gangbanging Karen when you were locked up. I walked in and seen it with my own eyes. Jay, you know I won't lie to you. Karen ain't the innocent little girl that she used to be. Come on, let that shit go. Ya'll killed his mother. Don't you think that's enough suffering for him?" Mally G said, putting emphasis on "enough."

"Aight, look. After I kill Brazy Boy, I'll squash the whole beef, but if I catch Will out of pocket, he dead too. I don't give a fuck if he raped her or not. He the reason she got shot!"

"Aight, fuck it, that a do. Call ya lil squad off before one of them get hurt. I'm about to bring Brazy Boy to Prince Street Projects. Meet me in front of building 158 in five minutes."

"Say no more!" Mally G walked over to where Na Na, Simba, and Brazy Boy were standing. "Yo, take this ride with me."

Once he got into the vehicle, he asked, "Where we going?"

"We bout to meet this gun connect in the projects real fast. I want to grab some extra guns just in case this beef get out of hand."

"Trillz, that's what's good, big bruh."

Mally G drove straight to Prince Street Projects and parked in front of building 158. Moments later Jay pulled up alongside of them.

"Come on, my man right there," Mally G said before they exited the vehicle.

Jay and him never saw each other before which made him not even think twice. The three of them walked into the building. While they were walking up the stairs, Jay drew a gun from his waist. His eyes got wide and his heart started to race.

"What's cracking now, bitch!"

"Word! Mally G, you gone really set me up?"

"Let me see!" Mally G said before he took the gun from Jay's hand**.** **Pow! Pow! Pow!** Three headshots sent his body crashing into the floor. "You shot my sister, pussy!" **Pow! Pow!**

Mally G shot his lifeless body two more times before him and Jay fled the scene. When they got outside, they shook hands as Jay said, "I love you, bruh. I knew you wouldn't cross me."

Chapter 14: Menace's Trial

Two weeks later:

Menace felt as though his case was weak and the prosecutor didn't have enough evidence, so he told his lawyer to push for a speedy trial. His lawyer told him it would be a good idea to rush the prosecutor so they would be unprepared. He was also tired of sitting in jail, so he wanted to get the process going as quick as possible.

It was finally the time to find out who is the confidential informer, and to find out if Menace would be released or have to do hard time in prison. Menace told Mally G and all his close friends not to come to his trial because it will look bad in the eyes of the jury to see a lot of street-type people coming to support him. He wanted to use the role of an innocent schoolboy, so he had to play his role to a tee.

*****

"All rise for the Honorable Judge Shahida Garrett!" the bailiff announced before everybody stood up.

"You may please be seated," the judge said as she took a seat herself. "Good morning. We're on the record case number 253-730, the State vs. Tyrone Watson. All parties are here and present."

Menace was nervous as he ever been. He felt beads of sweat running down his armpits already, and it hadn't been five minutes into his trial.

He was dressed in a navy-blue tuxedo with a white collared shirt and a blue and white tie. He felt uncomfortable as he sat there with his hands folded in front of him on top of the table.

The lawyer and prosecutor went back and forth with motions and dispositions for an hour about who stays and leaves the courtroom. After the judge came to a conclusion, she brought out the jury and explained to them what they were expected of and how they should conduct their duties.

"At this time, we may proceed," Judge Garrett said as she nodded towards the prosecutor.

"Your Honor, my name is Regina Kearney. I'm the prosecutor representing on the behalf of the State of New Jersey."

"Your Honor, my name is Sherry Dot Counts from the law firm of Counts & Bryant's. I am here representing on the behalf of the defendant, Tyrone Watson."

"Mrs. Kearney you may proceed with your opening statement."

The prosecutor stood up, cleared her throat, and began. "Today we are brought here because a child was murdered by the defendant and his family deserves justice. Tyrone Watson is a well-known gang member who's affiliated with the notorious Blood set, Sex Money Murder. There's no coincidence that the set he's affiliated with involves the word 'Murder' because Tyrone is a murderer! He's what we consider a gangster! Gangsters kill and harm people because their superior gives them orders to do so, or because they feel disrespected and take matters into their own hands.

"Well this gangster named Tyrone Watson took matters into his own hands and brutally shot and murdered Tony Richardson, a 14-year-old child. He murdered him in cold blood! The only logical explanation anybody could come up with to why Tony was murdered was because he looks like his older brother. However, Tony's brother resembles him but it's evident that they are two different people. Tony's brother Farod is thirty-two, so it's almost impossible to get him confused with a 14-year-old child. So this means one thing—the killer knew exactly who he was murdering, an innocent child! He murdered an innocent child out of cold blood to get revenge on his brother.

"The forensic analyst determined that Tony was murdered at close range, meaning the killer got a close view of his target. Tyrone stood over little Tony's body and shot Tony until there were no more bullets in his gun. Tony was shot several times in the head." She paused and shook her head to let her words digest before continuing.

"Ironically Tyrone's gang brother's call him Menace, and I agree he is a menace to society. He should be in prison for the rest of his life. Families have been hurt because of people like Tyrone, and I believe the streets are much safer with him incarcerated.

"Tony's mother Linda came to her front door seconds after her son was murdered and witnessed Tyrone running towards his awaiting vehicle. Do you know how devastating that must've been to see your youngest child lying on the cold pavement lifeless while the killer runs off smiling? Well that's what Linda had to endure!

"Tyrone's own gang brother that witnessed the murder firsthand will be testifying on the state's behalf. He will tell us everything that happened the night of Tony's murder and what lead to the ending of a young child's life.

"Tony was only fourteen, with the dreams of becoming a football player. This year was his first year in high school, and he was so excited about playing freshmen football. His mother told me how he would always talk about how he would become a famous star and get her out of poverty. All his dreams and hopes are ruined now, all because Tyrone wanted revenge on Tony's brother.

"Tony, an innocent child, is dead because he was being a good kid and was taking out the trash for his mother. As long as Tyrone's a free man it's not safe for kids to take out trash! Nothing further your honor."

"Ms. Counts you may proceed with your opening statement," the judge said before Menace's lawyer stood up.

"Tyrone Watson, the child sitting here next to me is the total opposite of the picture Mrs. Kearney just painted. Tyrone is a victim in this case just as well as Tony. He has been falsely accused of a terrible act that he would never commit. Tyrone is innocent and is being framed by gang members that are looking for less time on pending charges they are now facing. You will see that the state had no substantial evidence. This entire case is built around lies and hearsay.

"Tyrone is not this monster the State makes him out to be. Tyrone is a 17-year-old child enrolled in Malcolm X Shabazz High

School. In my hand is Tyrone's last report card: A, B, B, A, B, B, A. Tyrone is an honor roll student with dreams of going to college and becoming a teacher. He is not affiliated with any gangs and never has been! He is a young law-abiding citizen with a plan to help better our community.

"His mother Tareesa Watson, a teacher at L.A. Spencer Elementary School, and his father Mark Watson, whom is a pastor at Hopewell Baptist Church, raised Tyrone. Tyrone grew up going to church his entire life and is a devoted Christian. He has been falsely accused of a terrible act that no God-fearing man will ever commit. He attends bible study every Saturday and sometimes helps his father run the services. Does that sound like somebody that will kill a child cold-heartedly? No! It's apparently clear that we have the wrong person here today on trial fighting for his life.

"Just imagine being falsely accused of a horrible crime such as murder when you know deep in your heart you are innocent!" Ms. Count stopped and turned her attention to Menace whom was well dressed and looking innocent with his hands folded in front of him before continuing. "Well, this young man right here is going through that exact scenario right now. He is innocent, and you will all see that soon.

"Of course, gang members will lie and say he's affiliated to save their own butts! Of course, they will lie and say he killed someone to save their own butts! So, of course, they will lie under oath to get a deal from the prosecutor to save their own butts! These witnesses that claim they witnessed a crime really witnessed nothing! It's very clear that they're only here to save themselves!

"Tyrone was not present when Tony was murdered and has no knowledge of the incident. He was never physically seen at the crime scene, and there is no DNA to link him to it. The State doesn't even have a gun or any physical evidence to link him to any of this. There's no question of if he committed murder or not because based on the evidence, it's clear he's innocent! The question at hand should be, 'why are we here in the first place and not out looking for Tony's murderer?' Nothing further your honor. Thank you."

*****

One hour later:

After the break the Judge looked towards the jury and said, "Good evening, everybody, and welcome back. During the one-hour recess did any of you have conversations with each other or anybody else about the case? No hands are being raised. Did any of you read or listen to anything on the radio that pertains to this case? Okay no hands are raised. Did any of you get on any social sites, tweet, talk, or blog about anything that pertains to this case? No hands are raised. Okay, Mrs. Kearney, you may proceed."

"Your honor I will like to affix this statement in the case. Initially, we had three witnesses when this case began. Unfortunately, one of our witnesses, Nykir Smith aka Na Na, was found shot to death two weeks ago at 158 Prince Street. I would still like to proceed with his statement as evidence in this matter."

"Your request is granted, please proceed."

Mrs. Kearney read Na Na's entire statement out loud as everybody listened quietly.

When she was done, Ms. Counts made the statement look like nothing. The whole statement was based on hearsay. Ms. Counts painted a picture about how rumors get spread and switched up from person to person. The statement actually worked in Menace's favor, being as though his defense was that desperate gang members looking for an escape route were framing him.

*****

"Mrs. Kearney, you may proceed."

"On behalf of the State, I would like to call on my first witness, Linda Richardson."

Linda walked up and got behind the stand, the bailiff swore her in before Mrs. Kearney began.

"Ms. Richardson, for the record who are you?"

"I am Linda Richardson, the mother of Tony Richardson."

"Okay, were you there when Tony was murdered?"

"I wasn't right there. I was in the house, but as soon as I heard the gun shots I ran to the window."

"Could you tell the court what you saw when you got to the window?"

"When I got to the window, I saw my son laying on the ground bleeding and a guy was running to a gray car."

"So you saw the guy who murdered your son before he got into the car?"

"Yes I…"

Menace's lawyer jumped to her feet and cut Linda off. "Objection your honor, Mrs. Kearney question was leading and suggestive!"

"Objection sustained. Mrs. Kearney, please rephrase your question," Judge Garret said.

"Did you see the person who shot your son before he got in the car?" Mrs. Kearney asked.

"Yes, I did," Linda answered.

"Do you see him in this court room right now?"

"Yes, he's right there!" Linda said while pointing towards Menace.

The prosecutor walked over, put her hand over Menace's head, and asked, "Are you referring to him?"

"Yes," Linda answered in a low tone.

"No further questions, your honor."

"Ms. Counts you may proceed," Judge Garrett said.

Menace's lawyer stood up and cleared her throat. "Ms. Richardson on the date of 9/20/2000, the date that your son was murdered, did you give a statement to the detectives that arrived on the scene?"

"Yes," Linda answered.

"In your statement you said that by the time you arrived to the window the shooter was running back to his car. Is that correct?"

"Yes."

"So you never saw the shooters face when the incident occurred? Am I correct?"

"Yeah, but the detectives said he did it! He killed my baby!" Linda screamed towards Menace while crying hysterically.

"So, basically, the only reason you're saying Tyrone Watson murdered your son is because the detectives told you?"

"Yeah, I saw him running towards the car!"

"But you never saw his face is that correct?"

"No, but I know it was him! They said it was him!" Linda said in between sobs.

"No further questions your honor," Ms. Count said before heading back towards the defendant table.

"Ms. Richardson, you may step down please."

*****

Last day of trial:

Menace was feeling good so far because the trial was going in his favor. Cops, Special Examiners, and Forensic Specialist all took the stand one by one and got annihilated by his lawyer. With one witness left and his lawyer on a winning spree, he felt as though it was no way possible that he could lose.

But that was only until the prosecutor said, "I would like to call my final star witness Wilson Dopson to the stand."

What the fuck is this nigga doing here? Menace thought when Wilson got on the stand. Menace shot him a cold stare, but Wilson frowned, and then matched his cold stare. Menace couldn't believe what was taking place. One of his close homies who knew too much was taking the stand on him.

After the bailiff swore him in the prosecutor began, "Wilson, how long has you known Tyrone?"

"I've seen him around since I was a kid, but I've known him personally for about a year and some change."

"How did you two meet?"

"We're Blood, I met him through his big homie. I'm from High Street, and he's from Astor Street. That's right down the street."

"Do you and Tyrone hang out together?"

"Yes, we cool."

"What do you mean by the term 'cool?'"

"You know, we be chilling with each other. We're like friends."

"What do you and your associates call Tyrone?"

"We call him Menace."

"Can you tell us the reason why Tyrone would be referred to as Menace?"

"Well the Big Homie named him that because he used to be doing some crazy shit—I meant stuff."

"Can you elaborate on what you mean by 'crazy stuff?'"

"Well stuff like… Umm he stay strapped all the time, and he be quick to get it poppin."

"Can you explain to the courts what that terminology means?"

"He always got a gun on him, and he the first one to pop off if it go down. You know what I'm saying."

"Could you tell me what happened on the day of September 20, 2000?"

"Me and Menace—I mean Tyrone—was riding up Sheppard Ave, and he told me to pull over. I didn't know why he wanted me to stop, but I stopped anyway. Next thing I know he jumped out with a gun in his hand. I told him to chill but he kept going.

"Some kid was walking out the house carrying garbage, and he started shooting him. The kid fell. and he kept shooting him. I was scared that if I left him that he would find me and kill me next so I waited for him. I asked him why he killed that lil boy, and he said his brother Finisher killed one of our homies."

"Do you see the person you're referring to as Menace in the court room right now?"

"Yeah, he's right there with the funny looking suit on," Wilson said as he pointed to Menace.

"Do you know who Nykir Smith is?" Mrs. Kearney asked.

"Yeah, that's Na Na real name."

"Can you tell the courts who Mr. Smith is and what happened to him."

"Well Na Na was one of our homies. He gave a statement on Tyrone, and Tyrone told our homies. They killed him so he wouldn't testify."

"Are you saying another person is dead because of Tyrone?"

"Yeah he called out there and told the big homie that Na Na was snitching so they killed him."

"No further questions, your honor."

"Ms. Counts, you may proceed with your cross examination."

Ms. Counts was at a loss for words for a few seconds. However, her aim was to impeach his character, so she cleared her throat and began.

"Mr. Dopson you've been arrested seven times as a juvenile and three times as an adult. And that's not including a pending shooting charge, am I correct?"

"Yeah, you right, but what that gotta do with anything?"

"Did you get offered any deals for testifying today?"

"Yeah, they offered to take ten years off my twenty years that I'm facing for the shooting. But he really did kill Finisher's brother! I was there, I seen the whole thing!"

"So if you didn't have Tyrone to testify against, would you have to do twenty years in prison?"

"He killed that little boy and got Na Na killed. He belongs in jail!"

"Can you please answer the question!"

"Yeah, you happy?"

"So you're only testifying to get less time?"

"I'ma keep it real I wouldn't have snitched if I wasn't facing my charges, but he really did kill that lil boy!"

"In your testimony you said you was the getaway driver to this murder is that correct?"

"Yeah I was driving, but—"

Ms. Counts cut him off. "So your telling me that you and Tyrone are both Blood brothers, ya'll are friends, but he didn't tell you he was going to murder someone?"

"Yeah, I ain't know he was gone do that shit!"

"The night of the murder where were ya'll going, since ya'll wasn't going to commit a murder?"

Wilson got stuck because he wasn't prepared for that question. He was looking in the air as if he was trying to remember.

"Where were ya'll going?" Ms. Counts repeated with authority.

"I don't know! I forgot! Damn!"

"Do you use drugs, Mr. Dopson?"

Wilson frowned and replied, "hell no!"

"Do you use alcohol?"

"Sometimes."

"Did you use alcohol the day you claim you committed these crimes with my client?"

"No."

"Well in your statement you said other wise, and you also admitted to using marijuana. So are you lying now about not using drugs and not being drunk during the incident, or were you lying then?"

"Aight I was a lil drunk that day, but I remember everything clearly! And weed ain't no drug!"

"Mr. Dopson you stated you were at the scene the day Tony was murdered, am I correct?"

"Yeah, I was there."

"Can you tell me the color of the house you claim you saw Tony come out of the day he was murdered?"

"I don't remember! I wasn't paying attention to no house!"

"Nothing further, your honor," Menace's lawyer said as she walked back towards the defendant table and winked at Menace.

"Mr. Dopson, you may step down."

★★★★★

They took an hour recess to prepare for their closing statements. Menace knew his freedom came down to how convincing his lawyer closing statement was. He had faith in his lawyer, so he was calm as he sat and waited to hear what his lawyer prepared.

"Ms. Counts, you may proceed with your closing statement," Judge Garrett stated.

Menace lawyer stepped into the center of the courtroom as if she was Beyoncé about to perform in front of millions. She cleared her throat then began, "As you all can see, this entire case was built upon hearsay and lies. Their star witness is a gang member that's facing time and would do anything to save himself. His credibility is inaccurate, unconvincing, implausible, and unreliable! There's no way we can send an innocent young boy to jail based on a bunch of lies. As you saw he didn't remember if he was drunk or not! He believes marijuana is not a drug, and this is the states key witness. This is who they rely on without any sufficient evidence!" Ms. Counts stopped and turned towards the jury.

"Let me paint two pictures for you so we all can see who we are dealing with. One, imagine being a God-fearing 17-year-old honor roll schoolboy who dreams of helping better his neighborhood. Now, imagine your entire life changing from heaven to hell because someone falsely accused you of the worst crime ever. Imagine having to question the God you served for so many years because you don't understand why your life changed so drastically! Imagine having to fight for your life on trial when it wasn't enough evidence to convict you in the first place! Imagine having to be incarcerated while going through the process and being treated like a convict when you know deep in your heart that you're innocent! Well if you can imagine that, then you know how my defendant, Tyrone Watson feels right now!

"Now on the other hand, imagine being a gang member, slash gangster, slash manipulator who is facing twenty years for attempted murder. Imagine the prosecutor coming to your cell and telling you she can make half of your time disappear if you testified and lied on a person you don't care about. Imagine you being selfish and not caring about anybody but yourself, so you take the deal. Imagine coming to court and lying to the jury, judge, and everybody present to save yourself. Imagine getting caught in your lies but you continue to lie despite what's obvious. If you can imagine that then you know how the states star witness, Wilson Dopson, feels.

"It's clear that Tyrone is an innocent child who is being falsely accused of an act that he didn't commit. The state has no evidence, no reliable witnesses, and no case. Why are we here? Why are we wasting our time here? Guilty without a reasonable doubt is what the prosecutor has to prove!" Menace lawyer paused and focused her attention on the jury as they listened attentively. "There is so much lies, deceit, and doubt in this case that it should take no time to draw the conclusion of not guilty! Thank you. Nothing further, your honor."

"Mrs. Kearney, you may proceed with your closing statement."

"Tyrone aka Menace is a menace. His own gang brother witnessed him murder a little boy in cold blood and shared it with us. Yes, our witness is a convicted felon. Yes, he forgot that he was drunk. And yes, he is not well educated. But he knows what took place. He knows who Tyrone is and was there when he killed an innocent child.

"When a person lies, it's usually little or no details. As you can see, when Mr. Dopson described who Tyrone is and why they call him Menace, it came out with ease. It was detailed and effortless! You know why? Because it was the truth! Mr. Dopson isn't on trial today so let's not focus too much attention on what type of a person he is. What I can say about him is he's the type of person that hangs out with Tyrone. 'Birds of a feather flock together' is how the old saying goes. So we have two gang members that are both into the same lifestyle.

"I don't know if you guys missed the expression on Tyrone's face when he saw Mr. Dopson enter the court room, but it sure wasn't the face of an innocent church kid his lawyer makes him out to be." The prosecutor took out a picture that was taken in the courtroom of Menace's face after seeing Wilson. He handed it to the jury, and then sat in silence as they passed it down until the last jury member saw it before continuing.

"That picture shows betrayal, shock, hatred, and anger. When you think you manipulated and beat the system, and then the person you committed the crime with comes in on the opposite side, you start to sweat like Tyrone is." The prosecutor waved her hand towards Menace so that everybody could see him sweating. The two-piece suit he was wearing didn't help the situation at all. Mrs. Kearney shook her head and continued.

"And please let's not forget about our other victim Nykir Smith. He gave a statement and was murdered because Tyrone told his other gang brothers that he was cooperating with the law. Is it a coincidence that Mr. Wilson knew exactly what happened to Nykir because he cooperated against Tyrone? Is it a coincidence that Nykir was brutally murdered days after his statement was released? And is it a coincidence that Nykir and Mr. Wilson were both gang members from the same neighborhood as Tyrone, and both told the same exact story of what took place? It's clear as air that these are not coincidences but are facts! The truth!

"Society is much safer with people like Tyrone aka Menace behind bars. If Tyrone gets released his next victim could be you or maybe your children. He didn't kill a rival gang member or a street kid. He killed an innocent child because he was related to his foe! This wasn't out of anger; it was pure evil! Only a maniac can kill an innocent person and continue on with life as if nothing happened. If we let him get away with this, I'm almost positive it won't end here. Another life and family will be torn apart because we let a beast out of his cage!

"Ms. Richardson lost her youngest child for no reason at all. I can't imagine the pain she's going through. All she wants is justice!

Is that too much to ask for?" She paused and looked at the jury as if she was waiting for them to answer. "Justice is all we want! Nothing further, your honor."

★★★★★

After hearing the closing argument, Menace didn't know what to think. For the most part he's been doing well the entire trial, but the end became shaky. The Judge's voice brought him back into reality.

"The court will take a short recess while the jury deliberates. Court is now adjourned," Judge Garrett said before she banged her gavel.

Everyone exited the courtroom. A correctional officer took Menace and put him in a small holding cell outside of the courtroom. His palms were sweating, and he was perspiring from being so nervous. His mind was racing. He had no idea what was coming next. One thing for sure he knew if he beat trial Wilson had to die.

He laid back on the hard metal bench as all kinds of thoughts ran through his mind. Hours passed, and he couldn't stop thinking. *Damn this nigga fucked everything up! I had trial beat by a long shot. That nigga credibility fucked up. I think I still got a chance. Please God let me beat this case. I swear I'ma try to change, I'll even forgive him for snitching on me.* Menace's thoughts ended once he heard keys rattling.

"Mr. Watson, come on it's time to see if you're going to heaven or hell," the correctional officer said, laughing as he unlocked the cell door.

When Menace came in the courtroom everybody else was already situated.

"All rise for the honorable Judge Shahida Garrett!" the bailiff said as everybody stood up while the judge came out.

"You may now be seated!" Judge Garrett announced before everyone took a seat. Then she turned towards the jury and asked, "Have you reached a verdict?"

"Yes, your honor."

"How do you find the defendant?"

"On count 1 of first-degree murder, we the jury find Mr. Watson guilty."

A small outburst occurred through out the courtroom before the judge ordered everyone quiet.

"On counts 2 of possession of unlawful possession of a firearm, we the jury find the defendant guilty."

Menace's heart dropped. He knew he would have beat trial if it weren't for Wilson. He turned his head and looked at Wilson who was seated in the first row and screamed, "Snub, I'ma fucking kill you, you rat!"

Chapter 15: Tough Love

Later on that day:

Menace losing trial and Snub snitching messed everything up in Mally G's life. Life was perfect. Everything was going good since he had killed Na Na by getting Jay to believe that it was Brazy Boy they killed. He killed two birds with one stone, the beef with Jay got squashed and he killed Na Na for snitching. Everything in Mally G's life was falling in place and now his big homie, slash friend, slash brother, slash street mentor had become a snitch. How could Snub really be a snitch? It just didn't make sense.

Through time and effort Mally G and India bond grew stronger. Since he ran into her at the club, he started spending a lot of time with her. He really felt like he found the right one. India was the first of girls that stayed the night with him numerous times without having sex with him. He tried every trick he knew, and she wouldn't budge. That only made him fall for her even more. He felt as though if he couldn't influence her to have sex with him, there was no way another man can once he got into a serious relationship with her.

She was unpredictable, and that kept Mally G chasing. She wasn't like the average girl who was so easy for him to read. She gave him a challenge, and that kept him interested. The only problem they had was her not willing to have sex with him without being in a committed relationship first. Mally G felt as though, why would he give up his freedom and girlfriends without knowing for sure if India was the one? But she would try to convince him all the time to let go and give them a chance.

"Jamal, I don't know how long you think I'ma sit around and wait for you to commit to me. You're not gone realize what you have until I'm somebody else's. You know how hard it is to find somebody that's not in the streets fucking everybody? I got ambition, I'm going to school, and doing something with my life, and you comparing me to these chickenhead bitches out here!" India became teary eyed. She wiped her eyes and continued, "I'm telling you, Jamal, I ain't gone sit around and wait for too long. I deserve better!"

"India, you have to understand that I'm not trying to hurt you! I really like you, but I know I'm not ready to be in a committed relationship. I don't want to mess up our friendship to be in a relationship. Most people force themselves into relationships because girls like you force niggas to get into shit they not ready for. I don't mind waiting until we're both ready. You gotta understand my point of view."

"Jamal, you sound stupid! You want me to wait around while you fuck all these trifling ass bitches and just act like nothing's wrong! If you're not ready to grow up and become a man, then that's on you! But I'm tired of sitting around with my feelings caught up waiting for you to see everything you want is right here. I'm not waiting no more, when you come to your senses let me know, but just hope it's not too late and another man have what could have been yours," India said before heading towards the door.

"Come here, India," Mally G said as he reached for her arm.

She pulled away and said, "It's nothing else to talk about!" Tears streamed down her face as she exited the house and slammed the door.

Mally G sat there staring at the back of the door wondering how this would turn out. His phone rang and brought him back to reality.

"Shice, what's popping, big bruh?" Mally G answered.

"Come on High a.s.a.p. We know who snitched on Menace."

★★★★★

One hour later on High Street:

Snub walked into the building as Shice, Mally G, and BG were talking about the situation. He had no idea they knew he took the stand on Menace because it had just happened earlier that day. Menace and BG's cousin called BG as soon as the trial was over.

She knew Snub's real name and described him to the tee. Also, she told him about the deal he took for the pending shooting charges Snub was facing, so BG knew she was telling the truth.

"What's poppin with ya'll?" Snub said as he peaced them one by one. They all kept their composure as if everything was normal. "Look at this ratchet One Pac gave me, this shit official!" Snub said excitingly while removing a gun. It was a black 17 shot 40 caliber with a rubber grip handle, a scope with a built-in beam, and three air holes on top of the barrel.

"Damn! That shit official. Let me see," BG said as he reached for the gun. After Snub handed it to him, he looked at it then placed it into his jacket pocket.

"Yeah aight, give me my bitch," Snub said while laughing.

"I ain't playing, fuck you! You trip-nined on my bousin Menace!" BG barked with a frown.

"What?" Snub asked with a confused expression.

"Don't play stupid, nigga! My family was at the trial. We know you took the stand to get less time, motherfucker!" BG barked.

"Oh, that's how you feel! Come on, snitches suppose to die. Take me in the back and kill me. I can't live like this. If I'ma snitch then kill me!" Snub barked back.

"Snub, get ya stupid ass out of here!"

"Nah, Shice. I snitched I deserve to die."

Shice pushed Snub headfirst into the wall. "Get the fuck outta here!"

Snub staggered out of the building and walked away as they watched.

"Shice, why you ain't let me kill him? You know Snub gone be a problem," BG said.

"It's gone hurt him more to live than to be dead."

Shice knew what he said was probably a lie. Deep in his heart he knew it would have hurt him more to kill Snub than to let him live.

"So, you saying we not gone kill him even though he snitched?" BG asked, looking confused.

"Nah, he food so he gotta go. Right now just ain't the right time. His time coming soon," Shice assured him.

Mally G just sat there in a daze thinking. *Damn this some crazy shit. How Snub gone snitch out of all people? He's the one that taught me to never snitch. He did say he wanna die cause he couldn't live life as a snitch. Fuck it, if he wanna die, I'll kill him. It won't hurt me as much knowing that's what he wanted anyway, and I promised Menace I'll kill who ever snitched on him. Snub probably went to his apartment on Spruce Street. Let me get this shit over with. Danm this shit crazy...*

"I'm about to see something real fast. I'll be right back," Mally G said before peacing them and walking off. He knew he had to kill Snub on the strength of Menace, so it was better to get it over with than let it linger on his mind.

★★★★★

Down Hyatt Court:

Jay walked in the house and saw Karen sitting on the couch watching television.

"Oh, Karen. I meant to ask you about something, but it slipped my mind. I need you to tell me the truth too. Karen don't lie either cause some of my homies told me how you be moving out here!"

"Jason, what you talking about?"

"Mally G told me when I was locked up that he caught you letting niggas gangfuck you. Now what the fuck happened, Karen?" Karen pulled her knees into her chest and started crying immediately. Jay shook his head and said, "don't start crying, you wanna be a lil hoe, right!" Karen just sat there crying but still didn't say a word. "You make me be ashamed of being ya brother. Ya hoe ass probably never got raped either!"

"He did rape me!" Karen yelled in between cries.

"How the hell you expect me to believe that when Mally G saw you fucking his whole set!"

"Mally G act like he ain't fuck too!"

"What!" Jay barked with evil in his eyes.

"Yeah, you heard me. He fucked me too!" Karen yelled as tears ran down her face.

"You a nasty bitch!"

"Fuck you, Jason! I hate you!"

"Bitch, I hate you too, you fucking hoe!"

Jay grabbed both of his guns out his draw and then slammed the door on his way out. *Mally G just keep crossing me. It's time for me to cross him for once!*

*****

Back on Spruce Street:

When Mally G approached Snub's door, he was so nervous that his hand began to shake. He came there for one reason, and he didn't know if he was ready for it. He took a deep breath and started knocking on the door… Knock! Knock! Knock! Knock! Knock! Knock!

Snub opened the door and walked into the back room without saying a word. Mally G followed behind him, happy he didn't have to face him just yet.

When Mally G entered the room, he started talking immediately to avoid from thinking. "What made you snitch on Menace?"

Snub sat in silence for a minute, and then he looked Mally G directly in his eyes and said, "Mally G you know I always been grimy, I ain't snitch on no bitch shit. I snitched on some grimy shit. I was facing a twenty with a eighty-five. That's eighteen years of my life, it was him or me. You only live once, and I can't see myself spending my only life wasted in jail. I'll rather be labeled a snitch than to go to jail forever and niggas forget about me anyway. If that was you, you know I wouldn't have snitched on you. I ain't grow up with Menace. It was him or me."

"What about the code of the streets?"

"Fuck them codes! Humans made up those codes. This is a cruel ass world. You a get swallowed alive if you follow them fucking codes! A real man makes his own codes! I don't feel like a snitch. I feel like I did what I had to do to protect me! I gotta look out for me cause nobody else will!"

"If you feel like that, why was you gone let BG kill you?"

Snub put on the most serious face that Mally G had ever saw before saying, "I was gone go in the back with him, ya'll was gone hear gun shots too. But ya'll would've came back there and found his ass dead, not me. I would've took my gun from him, and killed his bitch ass. BG know how I play. I don't believe he'll set himself up like that!"

"So what you plan on doing now?" Mally G asked curiously.

"I'ma go down south before my sentencing date, but a lot of niggas gone die before I leave. I know niggas gone be gunning for me once Shice say I'm food. Niggas should've killed me when they had the chance. Now it's on! You and Will the only niggas I could trust, everybody else could get it." Snub stood up and walked towards the window, and then he opened the blinds and started staring outside.

This nigga talking stupid, he talking about killing the homies. He gone fuck our set up. Why did it have to be Snub out of all people? Why him? Fuck it, I gotta do what I gotta do, Mally G thought. He stood up and walked up behind Snub, he still hadn't built up the strength to go through with it yet. *Fuck it! Once you pull out it's no turning back,* he thought, trying to convince himself.

As soon as his hand touched the handle of his gun Snub spoke. "Do you think Mar Mar knew he was gone die before he died?"

"I don't know. What made you ask me that?"

"Nah, I was just thinking."

Snub still was staring out of the window and never looked back. Mally G drew the gun from his waist then raised it to the back of Snub's head as his hand trembled.

"Mally G?" Snub said while still looking out of the window.

"What up," Mally G responded.

"You know I love you, right?"

A tear fell down Mally G's right eye before he said, "I love you too."

POW! POW! POW!

★★★★★

Later on that day:

Ring… Ring… Ring…

"Yo!" Mally G said into the receiver.

"Where you at?"

"I'm in the house, why what up?"

"I need to talk to you."

"Look, Jay, right now ain't the right time. I'm going through something."

"I'm going through something too. I really need to talk to you. It's important."

"Aight, where you at?"

"Meet me by Spencer. I'ma be parked on Summerset."

"Aight," Mally G said before he hung up his phone.

Jay took two more pulls of his dipped cigarettes of PCP before walking out of his apartment on Barclay Street. He smoked three dipped cigarettes by himself, so he felt like he was floating. He walked straight past his car and started heading towards Summerset Street.

"Mally G keep crossing me. He turned slob, he fucked my lil sister, he put his slob homies first! I gotta kill him! We suppose to be best friends. Best friends don't do shit like that. He the devil, and God want me to kill him. Right, God?" He looked up in the air while chuckling. "Answer me, motherfucker!" he yelled.

People were looking at him as though he had two heads as he walked down the street out bursting to himself. Tears began to run down his face as he shook his head and said "Why me God! What the fuck did I do to you?" He wiped his eyes with the back of his hand and began to laugh before he said, "I know why… Because I work for the devil." He began to laugh as though he heard the funniest joke ever told.

When he reached the corner of Barclay Street and Muhammad Ali Avenue, he drew both of his guns from his waist. "Ooooohh! I'ma kill this nigga! He crossed me God! Don't blame the devil this time, he crossed me! Nobody crosses Jay and get away with it! Nobody!" he yelled as tears fell down his face while he smiled and shook his head.

★★★★★

"Did you see that?" Detective Puller asked Detective Reddick.

"Hell yeah! That nigger had two guns in his hands."

Reddick picked up his radio and said, "This is detective Reddick from the robbery and homicide unit. Send back up on Muhammad Ail, in between Barclay and Summerset. It's a black male approximately 6 feet, thin, wearing a purple jacket and blue jeans. He's armed with two handguns."

"Roger, copy; all available units in the central area we have a suspect armed and dangerous on the hundred block of Muhammad Ali. All units proceed with caution."

Reddick pulled up alongside of Jay, then Puller exited the vehicle and pointed his gun at Jay.

"Freeze! Drop your weapons!" he yelled.

Jay was so high he just stood there looking at them. Moments later more police cars arrived at the scene.

"Drop your weapons, motherfucker!" Puller yelled again.

★★★★★

Oh shit! Mally G thought as he pulled up on the scene, seeing Jay surrounded by police with guns in both of his hands. He knew Jay was a little crazy, and he might do something stupid. He parked and walked towards the incident in hurry.

"Get back!" the policeman commanded when he saw Mally G approaching.

"That's my friend, I'ma talk him out of it! Please, don't shoot him!" Mally G yelled while still walking towards them.

"Jay, put the guns down! A couple gun charges ain't worth your life!"

Jay looked at Mally G and his eyes became wide.

"We supposed to be best friends! You crossed me too many times!" Tears were running down Jay's face.

Mally G was confused, the first thing that crossed his mind was that Jay must have find out about Brazy Boy not being dead. "Jay, I just wanted the beef to be over! Just put the guns down. It's not that serious!"

"You crossed me, motherfucker!"

POW! POW! Puller shot Jay twice as Jay tried to lift his guns up to point them towards Mally G.

Mally G's mind was discombobulated. He didn't know if he should be sad that his best friend got shot down in front of him, or happy that the police possibly saved his life. He had an idea why Jay said he crossed him, but he never pictured Jay taking it to that extreme.

Mally G was stressing so much from all the events of the day—from arguing and breaking up with India, to the situation with Snub, to this. The stress was so overbearing to handle, he passed out from a nervous breakdown.

Chapter 16: Romance

Nine months later in 2001:

Since then life had been great for Mally G, he felt as though he had been through hell just to get to heaven.

After losing two friends in one day, he realized it was no way possible he would lose India too. India was everything he been looking for in a girl and more. He had never loved anyone how he loved India. He took the chance and opened up and truly let her in. After experiencing love, he felt as though he had been missing out his entire life. He still had commitment problems as far as being faithful, but he never let any of his dirt make it back home. They were now living with each other in a big house that he brought in Maplewood, New Jersey.

Mally G still was supplying his old neighborhood with drugs while India was a sophomore in Penn State University. Her major was business management, so she helped Mally G run his laundromat and managed his money. Mally G had well over enough money to leave the streets alone and would promise India he would quit soon but never did. He had gotten accustomed to the lifestyle of having the finest things, but he had saved more than enough to quit and still live lavishly. But the fact of the matter was that he was addicted to the streets.

He really wanted to quit, and he knew what he had to do to get out. He explained to India how serious he was this time. He told her once he bought his mother this house he saw and introduced Brazy Boy to his connect, he was done for good. He had been training Brazy Boy how to run his drug business so once he got out Brazy Boy would take his place and everybody would still be happy. Brazy Boy would give him a small cut every week, but for the most part Mally G would be done. He had one more large shipment coming in before he was officially done for good.

★★★★★

Ring… Ring… Ring…

"Big bruh, what's poppin?" Brazy Boy said into the receiver.

"You already know! Look I'ma need you to take this trip to NC to meet the connect. Yeah, you the man now," Mally G said before laughing.

"How I'm supposed to get there?"

"I got ya plane ticket already, and the connect gone have a car loaded and ready to be driven back. I already told him you gone be the man now. I milked the game for what it's worth. It's your turn now!"

"Trillz! I'ma bome to ya house in a minute to pick up them tickets."

"Nah, I'ma hit you when I get to the hood."

"Trillz," Brazy Boy said before hanging up.

When Mally G turned his head, India was staring directly in his face looking disappointed.

"Baby, it's my birthday. I thought you was gone spend the whole day with me."

"I am. I just gotta handle something two-second style. It's your special day, and I promise I'ma make it an extra special day for you."

"Aight, Jamal. Whatever!" India said before walking into the bedroom looking upset.

Mally G grabbed his keys off the key rack and headed for the door. He drove from Target, to the dollar store, to the liquor store, then stopped on Route 21 and bought two dozen of roses. On his mini shopping spree, he purchased a CD player, an Avant CD, a red lightbulb, a bottle of Moet, Remy Red, and some Hennessey. He also picked up a blindfold, five vanilla Dutch's with five bags of Haze, and two champagne glasses. Then he made a stop on 1&9 Highway and dropped the plane ticket off to Brazy Boy on his way back home.

He picked India up and took her to Caroline's Comic Club in Times Square. They got there a little late, so they had to sit in the side rooms because the main room was packed to the fullest capacity. India still enjoyed herself. She was laughing so hard her stomach started hurting after one of the comedians said Mally G looked like a used tampon because he had on so much red.

When they left there, he took her to Tops Diner in East Newark. They both ordered shrimp scampi. They were full from the appetizers, so when their entrees came they picked through them and ended up wrapping them up to go.

"Come on, baby. I'm ready to go home," India said while rubbing her stomach.

"Nah, let's go to the Telly. I wanna sit in a Jacuzzi and relax my body."

"Okay, baby. That do sound good," India said with a huge smile.

They pulled up to the Benedict motel off 1&9 in Elizabeth. Mally G exited the vehicle and walked towards the check in area while India was in deep thought. *Damn, I love Jamal so much. My birthday couldn't have been any better. I enjoyed myself with the love of my life by my side. I did expect a materialistic gift like that bracelet I kept hinting for him to get, but its okay. Memories last longer.*

Knock! Knock!

India jumped when Mally G knocked on the window, scaring her as she snapped back into reality.

"Grab that brown bag out the glove department and come on," Mally G said after he opened her door then put his hand out to help her out of the car.

"What's this?"

"Open the bag and see."

"Oh my God, Jamal!" she said excitingly. "Where you get this picture from?" It was a picture of him and India standing next to each other in the second grade.

"I stole that picture off the bulletin board next to our class when I was seven years old. I swear I loved you since I first laid eyes on you. It was at my mother's house ever since. I went through hell finding that picture in my mom's basement."

"Where you get this pretty frame from? This the best gift I ever received because it have so much meaning to it." The picture was in a gold frame with "The Love of my life" engraved at the top.

"I got that custom made," Mally G said while smiling. "That's 14-karat gold by the way."

Once he opened the motel room door, her eyes lit up. "Oh my God, Jamal! I love you so much!"

She gave him a long tight hug and a kiss before walking in the room. It was a trail of rose petals from the door to the bed and petals spread all over the entire bed. The red light gave the room an illuminating aura, making the setting more romantic. The jacuzzi was filled with bubbles with a glass of champagne and a rolled blunt sitting on each side. There was a small table sitting near the jacuzzi with two tall cups and a fifth of Hennessy, Moet and Remy Red sitting on top of it. A CD player was sitting on top of the pillow with big earmuff headphones.

"When did you have time to do all this?" India asked excitingly.

"I told you I had to handle something earlier. Now get ass naked so we can hop in the Jacuzzi before the water get cold."

"Is it still warm?" India asked.

"Yeah the room keeper filled it up just before we came. So strip naked, and stop asking questions! Daddy got this under control," he said still smiling.

"Yes, daddy," India said with a flirtatious look before stripping naked.

Mally G bit his bottom lip softly and shook his head side to side. He sat and admired her body as she undressed. Even though he saw her naked plenty of times, he still admired her beauty.

India was beyond gorgeous. At 5'6" and 120 pounds, she was perfectly curved in all the right places. Her body was well toned, and she was slim but thick in all the right places. Her butt was plumped for her size with a cuff you could put two fingers under. She had a perfect set of C cups that sat up flawlessly, and small Hershey Kiss nipples the color of a strawberry smoothie. Her skin was that golden color of autumn leaves, and she had straight silky hair with a fresh doobie that hung down to the middle of her back. Her face favored Lauren London's with those deep dimples and innocent eyes, but her eyes were the color of an almond. She had long natural eyelashes, with neatly arched eyebrows and perfect teeth making her smile breathtaking.

They stayed in the Jacuzzi for about a half an hour while smoking and drinking. India only took about three pulls of her blunt before she duded it out. She didn't smoke, but she did it only to make Mally G happy and because it was her special day. She only drank on certain occasions, so after a couple cups of Remy Red mixed with a little bit of Hennessy she was feeling good.

Mally G reached down to the bottom of the Jacuzzi and came up with a diamond studded Gucci link tennis bracelet.

"Happy birthday, baby!"

"Oh my God, Jamal. I love this bracelet! I thought you forgot!" she yelled excitingly before she gave him a passionate kiss. "Baby, if you pull anymore rabbits out of your hat, I'ma pass out. My birthday was perfect thanks to you!"

"I was hoping you felt the bracelet yourself, that's why I put it on your side of the Jacuzzi, but you fucked up my plans," he said while putting on a fake sad expression.

"I'm sorry, baby," she laughed while rubbing the side of his face.

"Come on, I got one more surprise for you," he said with a smile before he took her hand and led her to the bed. "Lie down and put them headphones on."

She laid on her back and did as he said. He reached in his pocket, pulled out a blindfold and placed it over her eyes. She was smiling uncontrollably. She was lost in the moment. He reached over and pressed play on the CD player. Movements later her favorite song by Avant. *"When we make love"* started playing through the headphones: *"I got your legs spread all over the bed, hands clenching on the sheets, hair wild as hell I know, the only thing on your mind is sexing me girl..."*

He leaned down towards her love boat, spread her legs apart, and pushed them back to expose her goods. He placed his head in between her legs, spread her lips apart with two fingers, and then slowly let his tongue run laps around her love button. She started to moan vigorously as he spelled out each letter of the alphabet with his tongue. Her moans grew louder as he went on. “Uhhhh!! Uhhhh!!”

She didn’t realize how loud she was moaning because the music in the headphones blocked out all sound. Mally G heard her loud and clear and loved every bit of it because it told him he was getting the job done. He blindfolded her and put music in her ears to make his touch more effective. The way our senses are designed is if one is ineffective, the others will become stronger. She couldn’t hear or see so his touch became enhanced.

He softly sucked her clitoris and flicked his tongue up and down causing her to orgasm. Juices squirted out of her spraying him in his face as he centered in on her clitoris making her orgasm extra intense. Her moans went from moans to cries as she gripped onto the sheets trying to gain back control. He began smacking his lips together while they were wrapped around her clitoris. Her clitoris popped in and out of his mouth as she dug her fingers deeper into the sheets and cried moans of joy. He added tongue as he did it and knew it made a difference from the reaction her body language gave.

After a while, he stuck his tongue out as far as it could go and started moving his head from side to side as fast as he can. Her legs started trembling and she couldn’t take it anymore. She pushed his head trying to stop him from going further. He wrapped his arms around her thighs and locked her in position as he continued. She gripped his hair hard and released an inhuman type cry as her body liberated its juices on to his face.

His entire face from the nose down was dripping wet. India was still laying back, breathing hard when Mally G reached down to take the blindfold and headphones off her. He was smiling super hard from the expression she wore, he knew he done a good job.

“Baby, I’m going to sleep," she said in a low tone.

Mally G laughed then said, "Oh no you not!" before climbing on top of her.

He slowly inserted the head of his manhood into her wetness, and then pulled back out while softly kissing her neck. He repeated that for a couple of minutes teasing her. She wrapped her legs around him yearning for him to go deeper. He then slowly pushed his manhood deeper inside of her inch by inch until his full length was in her. He continued to long stroke her with a steady pace as she scratched his back and bit down softly on her bottom lip.

Loud moans of pleasure escaped her. "Uhhhhhh!! Uhhhhhh!! Daddy, it feels so good!! Uhhhhhh!! Please, don't stop!"

He continued to long stroke her for three more minutes, and then motioned for her to get on top. He flipped her over while still inside of her. She began to ride him as juices dripped down his ass from her wet pussy like a mini waterfall. She put her head back and closed her eyes while grinding back and forth on his stiff dick. Her pussy was so warm and wet that it gripped his dick like a tight velvet glove.

He cuffed both of her smooth soft butt cheeks and pumped harder and faster as he guided her body into his until her orgasm erupted again. Then she spun around with his dick still inside of her and got into the reverse cowgirl position. He softly bit his bottom lip as he watched her soft plump butt bounce up and down leaving a coat of pussy juice on his manhood. Her pussy was making a slurping sound and her moans grew louder as her pace picked up.

Slap! Slap! Slap! Her ass lightly jiggled every time their bodies met. He grabbed a hand full of her hair and pulled her head back as he pumped harder and faster. "Aahhhh! Uhhhh! Uh! Uh! Uh! Mally! I'm cumming!" she yelled as her pussy tightened around his dick.

He pumped about three more times before his orgasm came as well. His legs began to shake as his whole body shut down. He pushed as far as he could and leaned his chest against her back as he exploded inside of her.

They were both breathing hard as they laid there all sweaty and wet.

"You ready for round two?" he asked, in between deep breathes before laughing.

"No, in the morning. I promise. I'm drained," she replied.

Chapter 17: When Good Turns Bad

When Brazy Boy exited the plane, the connect already had somebody there waiting for him. To his surprise it was a woman, and she was brownskin and pretty. She waved him over as soon as he stepped off the plane.

"Ya name Brazy Boy, right?"

"Yeah."

"Follow me."

She walked off and he followed behind her. There was a black Lincoln Continental limousine waiting for them outside of the airport. She got in without saying a word as he followed.

"Ma, what's ya name?" Brazy Boy asked after he got situated in his seat. She ignored him and kept texting on her phone. "Damn, sexy. What, you don't like talking?"

"My name is Jamerica if you must know, and no I don't like talking. It's nothing to talk about. We're going to do business and that's it."

For the rest of the ride they sat in silence, she took him to a big house in Greensboro, North Carolina. There she counted the money, and then gave him some keys to a Jeep Grand Cherokee. She got in the Jeep with him and pressed a couple of buttons on the door panel. The whole dashboard lifted up, exposing about twelve kilos of raw cocaine and a handgun packed into the secret department. She showed him how to open and close the stash box then showed him how to use the navigation system.

"It's safer to leave in the morning. It's a couple of hotels a few miles down if you wanna get a room for the night," she said before getting out of the Jeep and walking away.

He took her advice and drove to a nearby hotel. He was sitting in the hotel room bored as hell. He had slept the whole plane ride, so he wasn't tired and it was only 10:00pm. He decided to drive around and look for a bar or club. He was lucky and found one not too far from his hotel room.

When he walked in the club all eyes were on him, his demeanor yelled "I'm not from around here!" He was starting to feel like a celebrity how all the attention was on him.

"You ain't from around here, are you?"

"Nah, I'm from Newark."

"Oh, you from New York!" she said excitingly.

"Nah, ma. Newark, New Jersey."

"Oh, you a Jersey boy, huh?" She said while staring in his face smiling.

She was gorgeous, and he felt awkward letting a woman so cute push up on him, so he reversed the situation. "What's your name?"

"My name is Jessica."

"Well look, Jessica, I'm in town for the night. I got a hotel room not too far from here. How about we go back to my room so we can get to know each other better."

"Look, give me your cell phone number, and I'ma call you as soon as I drop my home girls off."

"Aight."

He gave her his number and bought some marijuana from a guy at the bar. Then he headed back to his room. He was tipsy off five shots of Remy Martin. He didn't want to get too drunk. He knew he had to be on the road early in the morning.

He hadn't smoked low-grade marijuana in a long time, so the high felt different, and it gave him a slight headache. His head was spinning as he laid down on the bed staring at the ceiling. The sound of his phone ringing brought him back into reality.

"Brazy Boy hotline," he said as he answered his phone.

"What you doing?"

"Who the fuck is this?" he snapped not recognizing the woman's voice.

"Day'um! Boy, you ain't gotta wild out its Jessica, the girl you met at the club. I just dropped my homegirls off. What hotel you at?"

"I'm at the Day's Inn, the one right around the corner from the club."

"Oh, aight I'm about to stop at the store then I'm on my way. Do you want anything while I'm at Wawa's?"

"Yeah get me a Pepsi and an Advil. I'ma give you the money back when you get here."

"Don't worry about it, baby. I'ma call you when I'm outside."

Damn she pretty as hell. I'ma beat that pussy up. I gotta come back out here, I like how these bitches be coming.

Moments later, his phone was ringing. After recognizing her number, he went straight to the door and flagged her down. When she came in, he couldn't believe how pretty she was. She looked even better now that it was light to show her true features. He smoked a blunt with her then went straight in for the kill.

"Ma, I ain't gone beat around the bush because I gotta be on the road early in the morning. What you try'na get into?"

"Whatever you trying to get into," she said looking him up and down.

"Well do something to me to make me wanna come back."

She didn't even respond verbally, she just reached over and started unzipping his zipper. He leaned back and watched her go to work. His manhood was semisoft when she pulled it out. As soon as her warm mouth wrapped around it, it grew in her mouth instantly. She looked him square in the eyes as she slowly made his full length disappear and reappear like a magic show. He couldn't believe she did it so effortlessly without gagging or pausing. She continued to deep throat him as she picked up the pace. He felt himself about to cum and was relieved when she stopped and spit on his dick. She massaged the spit in with her hand before she ran her mouth down the side of his manhood.

"Damn baby girl," he groaned as she placed one of his balls in her mouth. She sucked each one softly and licked them as she watched his reaction. He was in heaven and her sex appeal only added a vision to the ecstasy feeling she created.

She started jerking him with all the spit her mouth accumulated while sucking the head hard. He couldn't take it any longer and released the most intensive orgasm he ever experienced. A sound escaped his mouth that sounded feminine as she sucked every drop or sperm out of is manhood.

She sat up and smiled before she licked her lips and asked, "Was that worth coming back for?"

He laughed before saying, "You made me moan like a bitch." He laughed again then continued, "Fuck worth coming back for, that was good enough to make me stay." They both started laughing.

Moments later he was sexing her like a porn star. She orgasmed eight times before he came once. After he was done, he went into the bathroom to take off his condom and clean himself off.

When he came back in the room, she was already asleep. He rolled another blunt and smoked half of it before he put it out. Once he was high again, all types of crazy thoughts started coming to his mind.

Damn this bitch pretty as hell, she pushed up on me, sucked my dick like I was her dude, let me fuck with no hassle the first night, and ain't want no money. This bitch ain't right. She probably try'na set me up. Fuck that! I'm about to grab that ratchet I saw in the stash box just in case this bitch try some funny shit.

Mally G always told the connect to put a brand new P89 Ruger with the package. He knew guns were cheaper down south, and he always wanted to be ready for the worst on his drive home.

Brazy Boy went to the Jeep and retrieved the handgun and placed it on his waist before going back in the room. He slept light with his hand close to the gun. He slept about five hours and woke up in the morning from the sound of her moving around. He pretended to still be asleep as he peeked at her with one eye. She was talking on her cell phone.

Who in the fuck could she be talking to this early? he thought to himself. He couldn't hear her that well because she was talking low, but he knew she was up to no good. It sounded like she said, "He lying down, come take his bread."

He grabbed the gun off his waist then sprinted to his feet. He pointed the gun at her. She dropped the phone and to him her facial expression read, "I'm caught".

"You stupid bitch! You'll never catch me slipping!" Brazy Boy barked.

Before she could utter a word, he shot her two times in the chest. POW!! POW!! He walked over to her and shot her one more time, then picked up her phone.

"Find another nigga to rob, I'm on point motherfucker!" he barked into the receiver.

"What! Where my friend at? What was that noise?" A woman asked sounding concerned. At that moment he knew he fucked up big time. She was telling her home girl he laid it down in bed, and he misunderstood her. He had just killed an innocent girl for nothing. Damn!

★★★★★

Back in Newark

"911 what's your emergency?"

"It's a drug house on 95 Brunswick Street. There's guns, drugs, and money in it. A guy named Mally G runs it with his two boys, Brazy Boy, and Simba."

"Who am I speaking with?"

Click! The line went dead.

★★★★★

Ring… Ring… Ring…

"Brazy Boy, what's good, bruh? Everything good?" Mally G asked.

"Yeah, I'm straight. Some bullshit happened, but I'ma holla at you about it when I get to the hood. It ain't nothing too serious, I just owe you a gun. I'm in Virginia right now but my man called me for 250 yams. I ain't try'na let that big sale go to waste. I tried to call Simba, but his phone keep going straight to the answering machine."

"Aight give me the nigga number, and I'll handle that soon as I drop India off."

Brazy Boy gave Mally G the number, and then Mally G said, "Hit me when you make it to the hood."

"Aight, big bruh."

Mally G called the number and set up a place where he can meet up with the customer and deliver the drugs. After that he dropped India off then headed to his stash house on Brunswick Street.

When he turned down Brunswick Street something looked suspicious. It was two tinted cars parked in front of the stash house that he never saw before. A crackhead he knew from around the way walked past Mally G's car shaking his head while looking suspicious. Mally G pulled alongside of one of the tinted cars and tried to look inside but he couldn't see anything through the dark tints.

He felt in his heart something wasn't right, so he decided to leave. When he went to pull off, he noticed a black Expedition with sirens flashing from the inside of it coming down the oneway street the wrong direction. He played it cool and pulled to the side to let them pass, but they cut him off. The two suspicious cars pulled up behind him, boxing him in.

They approached his car with their guns already drawn yelling, "Get out the fucking car!"

Mally G knew this wasn't a routine traffic stop by the officer's demeanor, but he wasn't worried because he knew he didn't have anything illegal in his car. He complied and opened his car door. They pulled him out of his car and placed him into handcuffs without any explanation.

"What I do officer?" he asked.

"Shut the fuck up!" Detective Puller said making him hit his head while pushing him in the back seat of the cop car.

Mally G was still calm, but his heart dropped when they took his keys and went straight to the stash house. He watched in disbelief as they came out with an half of kilo of raw cocaine, five hundred grams of crack cocaine, two P89 Rugers, a twelve gage shotgun, two scales, two Pyrex pots, and a bag full of empty baggies.

"We finally got your ass! Where the money at? Cooperate if you want to save yourself. Give me a name and address."

"Suck my dick! I wanna call my lawyer!"

Chapter 18: The Message

One year later 2002:

Mally G was facing fifteen years in prison, but his lawyer managed to get it down to a five flat. His fingerprints weren't on anything in the house except one Pyrex pot, and his name wasn't on the lease. The police impounded his car but said they found him in the house, so the case was kind of weak.

Mally G lawyer suggested that it was best for him to cop out to the 5 flat before the Feds picked up his case. He explained to him that it was a good deal for the amount of stuff he was arrested for. His lawyer also explained that even though he's taking a five flat he will be eligible for parole after doing a little over one year, and that it was a good chance he would be released because he had little to no priors. He also told him if he went to trial and lost, he would face up to twenty years, so Mally G took his lawyer's advice and copped out to the five flat.

When he finally left the county to go down state, he was relieved. He just wanted to start his bid so he could get it over with. The C.O.s at the county woke him up 3am and told him he was leaving to go to prison. He was happy to get out of the county and start his bid, but a part of him was uncomfortable because he didn't know what to expect next.

Once he got downstairs and the state transportation came, and he knew it was real. They were yelling and acting as if they were dealing with children. He felt like he joined the army. A skinny freckle faced white officer with chewing tobacco in his mouth walked up to the holding cell and slammed his nightstick into the bars.

"Play time is over! Whatever ya'll motherfuckers used to doing in this county stays there. You're in D.O.C. hands now! Line up. We gone strip search ya'll one by one and get ya'll on the bus as soon as possible. Anybody slow down this process, I'm a break your fucking legs and leave you here!"

The ride to the Central Reception & Assignment Facility (C.R.A.F.) was terrible. Everybody's hands were cuffed to handcuffs connected to a chain that came around their bodies and tight cuffs around their ankles making it very difficult to walk. Each chain gang held up to five people. The seats were made of hard plastic, and there was no room for your knees. The bus was hot, and the windows came down only far enough to let flies in. They also had black paint covering them so no one could see out or in.

The minute he walked into the facility, he had to strip naked again but this time in front of two correctional officers and about seven inmates. Mally G never felt so degraded and violated in his life. They searched him again while he was naked as if he created a weapon on the bus ride from the county. They made each inmate sit on a cold metal detector chair one by one before taking a cold shower.

During his stay there, C.O.s called him all types of names and violated him every chance they got. The thing that hurt the most was that he knew he really couldn't do anything about it. He saw somebody get cuffed and jumped on for staring at a woman C.O. too long. They made him disappear like he never existed after they brutally assaulted him.

Mally G couldn't believe he went from sleeping on a humongous comfortable king size bed to a mat a little thicker than cardboard and not even half the size of his one at home. He put his mat on the floor because it seemed to be cooler down there and then quickly changed his mind after seeing a mouse run past his cell.

Inmates were only let out of their cells an hour a day. His cell was located in the middle of the tier. He couldn't see the tiny television on either side.

But the part he hated the most about C.R.A.F. was the showers. They were only allowed out of their cells for a short period of time, so the showers would be packed. It was only two shower heads in a small area, so inmates would all be crammed up naked taking turns wetting themselves.

Every day they had him doing something different from seeing nurses to psychologists to dentists to teachers to classification. They finally classified him to Mountain View Youth Correctional Facility. When the C.O. told him to pack up because he was leaving the next day, he was beyond happy. C.R.A.F. was not a jail he wanted to be in.

So far, every stop was getting worse so he knew prison would be unpleasant too. When he got to Mountain View Youth Correctional Facility, it was the opposite of what he thought. It looked more like a beautiful college campus instead of a prison. It was separated by dorms with a humongous yard. He went to cottage 8, which was the intake cottage for all the people who first arrived.

Not even two weeks into his bid, he got shipped out for fighting over some guy from Trenton that was under his set. When he first went downstate, any problems that involved Sex Money Murda members, he was on the front line. They only shipped him out because the incident was gang-related, and they felt as though he would eventually become a problem on the compound.

After he lost a year of communication time and got a fourteen-month hit at the parole board, he realized he couldn't keep putting his freedom on the line for guys he'd probably never see again once he got home. Parole denied him because they felt as though he didn't get enough time for the charges he had and because the gang activities he was involved in.

He got shipped out to Northern State Prison and was on B-wing, which was orientation. From there he got sent to north side on C-wing. It was mostly older guys on that wing. He got put in a room with an oldhead from East Orange name Mukadean. They started off real distant from each other, but after a few days they began to talk and loosen up. Muk had fifteen years in and ten more to go before he even became eligible for parole. Mally G respected Mukadean's way of thinking. He never met no one so intelligent but still street.

One day, Mukadean walked into the cell and caught Mally G in deep thought. "What's on your mind, youngin?"

"I wanna go home!" Mally G laughed.

"You think you ready for the real world? What you plan on doing when you get out there?"

"I plan on getting that money. I'm try'na be rich before I die!" Mally G responded.

"So you going back to the streets, huh? Mal, I wish I had the opportunity to be your age again. You young. You gotta chance to achieve whatever you want in life, only if you use your mind and believe in yourself. The streets ain't the only way to get rich. Better yet, you'll never become successful messing with them streets. I wasted my entire life coming back and forth to jail cause I use to think like you. I thought I could outsmart a system that was here and designed way before I was even thought of. We're slaves in the mind until we get that life sentence that's waiting for us and become physical slaves. Have you ever heard of Willie Lynch?"

Mally G thought for a minute before saying, "Ain't that the slave master that used to lynch people?"

"Yeah, but it's much deeper than that. Let me put you on to some game. In 1712, Willie Lynch went around teaching the slave masters how to control and conquer black slaves by using fear, distrust, and envy. He figured out the only way to fully control blacks were mentally.

"One of the tactics he used was he would take the strongest, toughest slave and torture him as all the kids, women, and other slaves watched. It was to break the spirit of the ones watching. He would tie their arms and legs to opposite horses, light him on fire, and then beat the horses until they tore the man apart as everyone watched. Next, he would beat the remaining slaves until they were an inch away from death to install that fear in them. Then he would separate the light skin from the dark, and the old from the young, to create separation within us. Divide and conquer! He would tell the slaves if they ratted some one out for planning to escape, they would be free themselves. But in reality, they would be traded off to another slave owner to create the illusion that they were freed.

"That's part of where we get our selfishness from, and why we don't trust each other today. It was instilled in us since slavery and still affects us today. He bred those qualities into our DNA the same way we breed dogs for certain qualities today. Willie Lynch claimed that this technique would have an effect for thousands of years, and it still affects us today. Those traits carry on in our genes and the information is passed to our offspring the same way the toughness from fighting dogs get passed down to its pups.

"Not to mention the drug game was designed for us to be new generation slaves. The way we as blacks live was properly planned. We carry guns and kill each other because we fear each other, we don't trust our own brothers, and we hate to see the next person doing well. Those qualities have been instilled in us during slavery, and even though we feel like we're free, we're still mentally enslaved. One of Lynch's principles was 'keep the body, take the mind,' meaning break the will to resist. Us as black people accept poverty with no problem and don't even realize it's something wrong with our way of living. Lynch's plan was to focus on our offspring, our children, the future generation. Can't you see that each generation is getting worse? From judging our young generation in the streets, just imagine how their kids will be! This is no coincidence!

"Really, how do you think so much drugs get in and out of this country? The government allows that poison to come in so we can sell it to each other, kill each other with and over it, and so that they can lock us up and profit off it. That's one of the key things that break a black community. Just imagine the hood without drugs.

"They placed a black hole in the streets and we keep falling in it. Our people been falling in that same black hole for an eternity but still think it's a way to get around it. The only way to get around it is to go the other way, and that's legit! We have to let the love frequency into our hearts and let go of the hate. We can blame the government for some conditions, but we still have the opportunity to be what ever we put our minds to. As long as we think bigger than the streets, we can overcome this. We have options, unlike the slaves that were before us, and its time we wake up.

"Mal, let me ask you something. How many people you know personally or even heard of that got rich from the game without going to jail for most of their life?"

Mally G looked up while in deep thought. "Damn, none."

"If you think you're going to be the first, you're crazy! The streets are designed for us to lose. When brothers do make enough money to quit, they are so caught up in the lifestyle they never make it out. They get so accustomed to spending and making so much money that when they try to quit, life become too hard. You know what comes next; they turn back to the streets. When their drug business running so smooth and they feel nothing could go wrong, so why quit? How do the connect quit with so many people relying on them? They won't, but eventually somebody a get caught up, then snitching occurs, then everybody's locked up for life. It never fails!

"It's almost impossible to make the transition from a drug dealer to a businessman. There are laws such as tax invasion and money laundering that was made specifically for drug dealers. The minute you think about switching over, the Feds a be at your door with all types of charges. It hurts me to see ya'll young guys chasing a dream that's a nightmare in disguise."

He shook his head and laughed before continuing, "It's only an illusion! I wasted twenty-five years of my life to this system already. Fifteen years straight with ten to go, chasing that same illusion.

"Learn from my mistakes. A wise person learns from other people's mistakes, and dumb people keep going in circles because they're afraid if they change, they might become a better person, which the ignorant refers to as squares. Well squares don't come to jail. Squares become rich and stay rich. Squares out there getting pussy right now. I'd rather be a square than keep going around in this circle!

"I could tell from our conversations that you're smarter than the average Joe. Your wifey taking care of your businesses, you still got your house, and you still got all the money you milked the game for. You said you don't know anybody that got rich from the game that ain't go to jail for life, look in the mirror. Quit the game now and that could be your story. Do you know the difference between a liability and an asset?"

Mally G thought for a second before responding, "Nah, not really."

Muk shook his head and said, "If you really want to be rich, the first thing you have to do is learn about money, you have to become financially literate. How do you expect to become rich if you don't know how money works? That's like me saying I want to be an NBA player but never practice basketball. You see how people get big settlements or hit the lotto and wind up broke again. It's not because they splurged carelessly. It's because they don't know how money works. You gotta learn how to make your money work for you, so you won't have to work for money!

"Don't wind up like all the big time drug dealers that failed. ET Hak from Georgia King Village, Rasheem from Irvine Turner Boulevard., Dre from Astor Street, Sheek Ali from Haynes Home, Akbar Prayer from Prince Street, Mustafa from the Zoo Crew, and a whole lot of other good dudes from Newark had the same chance you got and blew it. Don't be the next statistic. Be better than them.

"The game messed up kid, ain't no more loyalty or love in them streets! If somebody don't kill you because they're jealous or because of some other dumb stuff, somebody gone snitch on you. This new generation doesn't respect the codes of the streets. Now a days you can't trust nobody in the streets. How many of your homies come to see you since you been incarcerated?"

"None, but I didn't ask none of them."

"Do you ask your mother when she come?"

Mally G didn't answer.

"Exactly! That's the difference between real and fake love. How many even write you? And don't add the ones that are locked up."

Mally G shook his head before saying, "None."

"That's how much the streets love you! I seen guys die in the hood. We got drunk, lit a couple of candles, got R.I.P. shirts, and it was over. We moved on like they never existed. It's true when they say the streets is cold. Do you want to be the next guy forgotten about?

"I'm only telling you this because I was you. I had enough money to leave the game and fucked it up. It eat me up to this day every time I think about it. I don't want you to feel how I feel now. It hurts to know I had the good life in my hands but chose this instead." Muk stopped talking and looked around the cell while motioning his hands before continuing.

"You see how a donkey get used to drag a cart? Somebody dangles a carrot in front of its face to manipulate it to work for them. Well, we get used the same way. We are the donkeys, and that lifestyle of fancy cars, big houses, and lots of money with a happy ending dangles in front of our faces. That donkey will never walk or run fast enough to catch that carrot, just like we will never get that happy ending. It's only an illusion. Keep that in mind and your reality will be much brighter.

"You can learn anything you wish but you have to use your mind. Make it your main objective! And the only way to do that is to give up and change what you used to do because the two don't coincide. It all starts with how you think. You can continue to think like a slave, or you can break the chains and be free! That's up to you youngin', your future is in your hands.

"I'ma give you one more important pointer to think about and I'm taking my old ass to sleep," Mukadean said while laughing. "The first step to change is making a decision. Remember, if you never make a choice, your choices get made for you. Making the decision is so important because it gives your brain a new direction. People conditioned mindsets have them believing it takes money and knowledge to make a decision, but that's a big lie! People put their goals and dreams to the side until the so-called right time come. But it never comes, and it never will. No millionaires woke up to that money without the groundwork getting put in first. Becoming a millionaire is a choice, but if you never decide to make the decision you'll never take the steps to achieve it.

"The only time we have is now, so it's about making the decision and following through until you've completed your goal. What you do now will eventually be your past, and what your doing now is also shaping your future, so in all actuality we only have now. It doesn't take money to make a decision, it doesn't take experience, it doesn't need to be a perfect time, all you need is the will to accomplish a task, and faith that it's possible. Before you go to sleep, think about the choices you need to take to get where you want to be, and reflect on how your old choices lead you to where you're at now. On that note, good night, my brother."

That night Mally G laid in his bed and thought about everything Muk was saying. He reflected on his life and thought about how crazy his life has become. His childhood best friend became his enemy, he killed Snub, the next closest friend he had, ZaZa and Mar Mar both was murdered because of choices he made, and he killed other black people for basically nothing. He realized that he did have a slave mentally because he accepted that lifestyle, and up until then never thought anything was wrong with the way he lived. He knew deep in his heart he had to change. He knew he wanted to change. He had a tough decision to make.

*****

One year later 2003:

"You have a Global Tel Link collect call from… Jamal Kelly… At Northern State Prison correctional facility. Hang up to deny the call, or to accept press 1 now."

"Mally G what's good, big bruh!" Brazy Boy said after accepting the call.

"Try'na get my mind right and get home to my family."

"Yeah, the family doing good, everybody getting money."

"Nah, I'm talking about my real family, my mother, my lil brother, and my wifey. The people who holding me down right now!

Other than you, don't nobody from the hood do shit for me. No letters, no money orders, don't put money on their phones, nothing!"

"You know how shit is in the hood, niggas gone hit you when you come home."

"That ain't love, niggas suppose to be there for me when I'm down too, not just when I'm up! Brazy Boy, don't believe them niggas really love you."

"No disrespect but on some real shit you talking some locked up bullshit, niggas love me and they love you too, big bruh! Niggas know you good. We out here tryna get the hood right."

Mally G knew it would be a process convincing Brazy Boy that the streets weren't right, especially over the phone.

"What my lil brother Amod be doing out there? My mother said he be hanging around ya'll now."

"Who, A-Wall? That lil nigga act just like you. You know he with the family right."

Mally G stood there in silence for a few minutes trying to digest what he had just heard.

"Who brought him home? I sent word to the hood that I didn't want him turning Blood!"

"Niggas was standing on High and Spruce, and he came up saying he ready to bum home. Everybody was telling him to chill, that you didn't want him involved. He started saying you wasn't his father, and he gotta live with the decisions he make not you. Then he told me to count, before I could respond he was swinging on everybody. They started swinging back, so I started counting. He family so he with us regardless, but he just wanted to be official. You told me you wouldn't never lead me in the wrong direction, I'm banging on the strength of you."

Mally G was at a loss of words for a moment. Brazy Boy took his own words and threw them back at him, and they felt like daggers to his heart.

Mally G responded, "I was lost like ya'll is, and I'm sorry I introduced you into this lifestyle, but believe me ain't no happy endings in the streets. Trust me!"

"Bruh, I trust you with my life, but you been gone too long and that shit fucking with ya head. You'll snap back into reality when you get out here."

"Ten seconds," the operator said.

"Brazy Boy, I love you, lil bruh. Be easy out there and just think about what I'm telling you."

"Love you too, big bruh."

*****

One year later 2004:

Mally G was reading as many books as he could trying to sharpen his mind. He started learning about real estate and began writing a book. He made plans to invest in building his own publishing company and one day publish his work.

India was holding him down with letters and visits every week. He loved her already but because she was there for him in his time of need, it made him love her even more. With everybody else it seemed like he was "out of sight out of mind," but India kept him alive. The parole board denied him parole two times. Almost three years passed, and India was still holding him down. She saw how much he had grown mentally over the years and supported him every step of the way.

A big smile came across India's face when she saw Mally G walk into the visiting hall. She'd been waiting forty-five minutes to see him. She went from checking in, to waiting to go to the back, to getting searched, then waiting another fifteen minutes before they brought him out. She jumped into his arms and gave him a long passionate kiss when he approached her.

"Baby, I miss you so much. I can't wait until you're home for good!"

"I can't wait either. I gotta make a little Mally G Jr.," he said before rubbing her stomach.

"I hope you're really serious about leaving the streets alone. We can't raise any kids with all the chaos going on out there. Plus, if you go back to jail, it's over. It feels like I'm locked up sometimes!" India couldn't imagine leaving him, but she told him that every chance she got to put it in his mind so he wouldn't go backwards.

"India, I'm done with the streets, nobody got rich and made it out the hood successfully. I'ma be the first. I got what I wanted out of the game, the game is over. It's my turn to try the other side. I've been in the streets my whole life and nothing seems to work, let me try the legit way maybe I will like it. My book almost finished too."

"Ooh, I can't wait to read it! And trust me you gone like it, baby. We more than good as far as money. The laundromat is doing excellent. I'm thinking about opening another one, so you could run one and I could run the other one. Plus, the publishing company, we gone be just fine," India said with a huge smile on her face.

"That sounds like a good idea that could be another asset added to our asset column. You can't become wealthy without building your assets," Mally G paused. His face brightened up before he said, "Oh! Baby, did I tell you that I got Menace moved into my room this morning? I ain't see my nigga in a long time. I can't wait to go back and holla at him."

"I talk to you every day on the phone and see you every week. Go and talk to your friend. Just make sure you call me."

"Baby, you bugging! He ain't going nowhere, me and Menace got all night to catch up. You drove all the way up here then had to wait hella long. I want all my visit time. I could barely sleep last night thinking about seeing you today. Now come here and give me another kiss."

After they kissed Mally G looked down at his pants and said, "Take ya ass back to sleep! It's not time yet."

India laughed before saying, "Stop talking to your dick. You know he hardheaded when it comes to me."

They talked for about another hour before the C.O. yelled out, "Visits terminated! All visitors must leave now. Inmates remain seated!"

Mally G hated this part of being incarcerated the most. Having to sit there and watch the love of his life leave always rubbed him the wrong way, and that's when reality kicked back in. Also, he hated that all the inmates had to get strip searched after every visit. As many times as he'd been to visit, he never became accustomed to stripping in front of a bunch of men.

"Hand me your boots… Hand me your pants… Hand me your shirts… Hand me your underwear, don't shake them or don't pop them… Put your hands out, turn them over… Let me see behind your ears… Run your fingers through your hair… Open your mouth, top lip, bottom lip and lift your tongue… Lift up your piece… Turn around… Left foot, right… Bend over and spread your ass cheeks."

He felt violated every time they did it.

When he got back to his cell a letter from his mother was sitting on his bed. He smiled then ripped it open before he sat on his hard bed and began to read:

Dear Jamal,

I miss you so much! I can't wait until you get home so you can do the right thing. A-Wall lil ass is becoming a piece of work. I need you home to get him back on the right path. You know he follow after everything you do. Jamal, I hope you're serious about changing cause the streets is only getting worse. You can't come out here hanging around the same people but expect to change. If you're serious about getting your life together you have to change the people you associate yourself with too. It's easier said than done, but the real test is when you get free. Son, I believe in you so come home and do the right thing. Your time is getting short so start setting your mind to leaving them old habits in the past. The family is good, and everybody send their love. I have to be at work in a few, so I'll write you again another time. Love you, son! Just keep in mind what I said. If you wanna change, you have to change your old behaviors.

P.S. I hope the 40$ money order helped.

Love Always, your mother

Mally G laid back in his bed and digested what his mother told him. He knew time was getting short, and he had to prepare himself mentally.

★★★★★

Just as he was about to drift into sleep, Menace entered the cell with his bags in his hand with a huge smile on his face.

"Damn. Mally G, you got big as hell, and ya dreads got long as hell too!"

"Shit, they don't sell this on commissary!" Mally G said while making his chest jump before they both started laughing.

"I thought they was been suppose to move you."

"Yeah they were, but I had to wait for Sergeant Eorio to do the paperwork," Menace replied.

"You heard my lil brother turned Blood?"

"Word! Nah, I ain't know that. I'm not in contact with nobody from the hood. I wrote Shice a couple times, but he never wrote me back. I know niggas be busy or something."

"Ain't no such thing as being so busy you can't write a five-minute letter. Don't make excuses for niggas!" Mally G said, feeling his pain.

"Mally G, real talk they gave me twenty years. I be feeling like I'm dead to the world. The only people that have been there for me is my family and this lil chick I use to fuck with. She a some-timer, but I can't complain. I treated her like shit when I was home. I'm lucky she even writes my ass."

"Damn that's crazy, all the shit you did for the hood niggas don't do shit for you?"

"Nah, I'm good, though. I got my family. I learned my lesson, and I ain't talking about from getting this time. I learned the difference between street love and real love. The only reason I'm in here is because I was riding for other niggas, all the beef I had started from other niggas. I turned Blood because I wanted to fit in with other niggas, but at the end of everything I'm in here doing 20 years by myself, not with other niggas. Mal, you about to be back out there, appreciate your freedom and live for you. You only get to live once. Fuck what everybody else think, and fuck what everybody else says! Whatever you do you gotta live with the outcome, not them!"

"I feel you, bruh. I'm coming home on some different shit, though. I'm done with the streets. This bid opened my eyes to a lot of shit, and I believe it saved my life."

Menace laughed and said, "I feel the same way. The crazy part is I never been as happy as I am today. Of course, I wanna go home, but I know God don't make mistakes. I'm thankful for everything, the good and bad. I finally made peace with myself and accepted who I am. God is so good, and he deserve to be praised."

Mally G was beyond shocked, "Damn, bruh, I swear I never expected to hear you talking like this."

Mally G thought Menace was going to be the same wild boy he used to be, but to his surprise he had matured. Now he saw the world for what it really was worth, he found his purpose in life. He always read the bible and the little scriptures his parents sent to him. He still was claiming his set but banged for a different cause. Menace believed in Mally G more than he believed in himself. He always told him he could make it legit as long as he stayed focused and put God first. Mally G wasn't that religious, but he took heed to everything Menace said and was happy it was all positive energy in their cell.

*****

One year later 2005:

Mally G max date was in the morning, he had been up all night because he couldn't sleep. He was nervous but anxious at the same time. He was focused and ready to go home and turn his life around. He had been through so much in life and learned so much. He learned the key to success in the streets was to get in and get out. He knew his little brother A-Wall, Brazy Boy, Will, BG, and Shice was going to make leaving the streets alone extra hard, but he also knew experience, staying focus, India, Menace, Mukadean, his mother, and the will to do good would make it easier. His mother always stuck by his side, right or wrong.

When they opened his cell and called his name to leave, he knew he was finally getting his freedom back. Whether he wanted to keep it or not was up to him. When he walked out of the prison, India and Shice were right there waiting for him.

Chapter 19: Can I Really Quit?

India was crying out of joy when Mally G approached them.

"I can't believe you finally home. It seems like I was waiting my entire life for this. Those were the longest four years of my life. I never want you to go back."

"Don't worry, baby. I'm never going back," Mally G assured her.

"What's good, lil bruh? Welcome home!" Shice said as he handed him a Gucci knapsack full of money.

"Good looking, big bruh, but I don't need your money."

"Nah, I don't want shit back. This from the set. What you want me to give it back to all the homies I collected it from? We were handling business out here making sure you don't need for shit once you're home. This a welcome home gift, do what ever you want with it." Shice put his hands in the air and backed up, letting Mally G know he wasn't taking the bag back.

Muk told me my fake friends would try to wheel me back in with money. Damn that bag looks full though. Fuck it! I'm still not getting in the game. I'll invest it into something legit.

"Good looking," Mally G said as he put the bag in India's car.

"Come on, let's get the fuck out of here!" Shice said while getting in the back seat.

"Oh, ya'll drove here together?" Mally G asked.

"Yeah, his car parked in front of the house. We met up this morning," India answered.

Mally G was in deep thought, staring out of the window as they drove home. Everything just didn't feel real yet. He didn't feel like himself. He felt somewhat uncomfortable. When they pulled up in front of his house and got out, he told India he would be in shortly he wanted to talk to Shice first.

"Damn, bruh, you don't understand how happy I am to have you back out here! You know the hood miss you, right? Everybody beasting to see you."

"Damn, where everybody was at when I was in that lonely ass cell stressed out?"

"You know how shit is in the hood, niggas try'na survive. The hood was fucked up for a minute when you left, now everybody eating. Shit running better than ever. You the reason shit running how it is, all you gotta do is sit back and collect grip. You ain't gotta put ya self on the line for the money. I got this shit mapped out. The lil homies on they bikes."

"Shice, I appreciate the love, but I'm done with the game. I'ma run my business and do the legit thing."

"You ain't gotta get your hands dirty, ain't no wrong in collecting money, you deserve it. Shit, you can do both," Shice said with a smile.

"Good looking but I'm good. If I ever change my mind about the game, you a know first. I'm bout to shoot in the house, though. I don't want to keep my baby waiting too long."

"Aight, love you, bruh. Welcome home, if you need anything holla at me."

"Aight, love you too."

Mally G knew things wasn't the same. He didn't get the same vibe from Shice as he did in the past. He knew he had love for him, but it felt like Shice's love wasn't genuine no more.

Mally G peaced him, and then walked into the house. As soon as he got into the house, India told him his mother and little brother were on their way.

"Damn, we can't get no privacy. Let's get a quickie in before they get here," Mally G said with a huge smile.

"No, baby, they on their way. Don't worry we got all night and the rest of our lives to be nasty."

*****

Ten minutes later his mother and little brother was walking in the house. He gave his mother a tight hug, and then went to shake his brother hand. But A-Wall tried to peace him.

"Damn! What, you ain't banging no more?" A-Wall said with a frown.

"Nah, I'm just not used to peacing your lil ass."

"Well get use to it. I'm Murda!" A-Wall said while holding both of his hands in the air shaped like guns.

"Amod, cut that shit out!" Amirrah yelled.

"Amod, let me holla at you on the side."

"Don't nobody call me Amod except for mommy. My name A-Wall," he said while following Mally G into the backroom.

"A-Wall, I want you out the streets. I'ma let you run this other laundromat that I'm about to get. The streets fucked up. I don't want you getting caught up in that bullshit."

"You been gone too long, the streets ain't fucked up. Niggas getting rich. I ain't try'na be making no pennies working at no laundromat!" A-Wall said while frowning.

"If you get it running good then it's yours. You'd be the youngest nigga with your own business. If you stay in the streets you gone end up getting caught up."

"Big bruh, that's that jail talk. You'll be back after a few weeks home. I don't know about you, but I love my hood. Don't let a lil time get you on no mushy shit. The hood could be yours. Niggas respect you more than they respect Shice."

"Fuck what niggas in the hood think! They don't give a fuck about me or you!"

"You talking some straight bullshit. Holla at me when the old Mally G come back. Most niggas come home on they Martin Luther King shit, but you'll be back soon."

A-Wall walked away smiling as he shook his head side to side. At that moment Mally G knew changes was going to be harder than he expected.

*****

One hour later:

"Damn, baby, I thought we wasn't gone never get no privacy. My mother know how to talk up a storm. Come here, we gone start right here in the living room," Mally G said while smiling.

He was sitting on the couch. She came over and straddled across his lap while facing him. He started kissing her as he gripped both of her soft cheeks in the palms of his hands. He got an erection immediately.

"Baby, I want you to suck the first one out of me."

She didn't say a word. She got onto her knees in between his legs and started unbuckling his pants. When she pulled his manhood out, he had pre-cum on the tip of it.

"I see somebody was excited," she said in between laughs before she placed him into her mouth.

Oh my God, this shit feel so good. Her mouth was so warm, and it felt like she didn't have any teeth. His erection was harder than ever, and the pleasure of giving him oral sex was making her wetter downstairs. She was performing like Superhead.

"Damn who taught you this?" Mally G asked jokingly.

"Jamal, don't play with me," she responded quickly with his manhood in her hand.

"Nah, baby, I was just fucking with you," he said while laughing. She continued where she left off, causing his toes to curl. Two minutes later he was yelling out, "Baby, I'm about to nut!"

She kept sucking, and he exploded in her mouth. She sucked until his orgasm was over causing him to moan as his eyes rolled to the back of his head. She stood up and ran to the bathroom. He knew she only kept sucking while he was cumming because he used to tell her how good that felt in letters that he wrote while incarcerated. He knew she hated the taste of cum, but she did it only to please him.

"That shit taste so salty and nasty. I don't think I could do that again. I heard if you eat pineapples that it tastes better."

"What took you so long though? What, you was in there throwing up?" he said while laughing.

"No, I had to brush my teeth."

"Come on lets go into the bedroom so we could finish what we started," he said as he took her hand and led her to the back.

"It's your turn now, I want you to sit on my face," she giggled as they walked.

They both stripped ass naked before he laid back on the bed. She saddled across his face with her hands and knees on the bed. Her pussy was clean shaved. When her legs spread across his face, the pinkness from her pussy grabbed his full attention. Her clit was peeking out from her pink lips. He placed his mouth around her clit and sucked softly causing her body to shiver. Light moans escaped as she began to grind on his face.

"Uhhhhh!! Oohhhh, baby!!"

He gripped her ass cheeks and started moving his head left and right as his tongue irritated her clitoris. Within no time her body trembled as her orgasm ran through her body. His face was covered with her love juices when he came up for air.

"Come on, baby. I wanna feel that dick inside me," she moaned.

She got on top of him and started rubbing the head of his manhood up and down her clitoris, teasing them both. Then she inserted his head into her tight, hot, wet pussy. She took her time as she eased up and down. From the lack of sex, her pussy was extremely tight. The wetness helped, but it felt like she was losing her virginity all over again. He groaned as she slowly grinded up and down. He could feel the wetness and the way her love muscle gripped his manhood so firmly. *Oh my God, I'm really in some pussy. This shit feels so good.*

"Uuuuhhhh... Baby... Ooooohhhh... Oh... My... God!!"

He gripped both of her cheeks as he guided her up and down. *Oh shit, nah it's too soon!* he thought while feeling his orgasm ready to explode.

"Baby, I'm about to nut. Uhhh!!!" he groaned while exploding inside of her.

"Baby, you gotta build your stamina back up," India said before chucking.

"I know. That's why we about to go for round two!"

Chapter 20: Blast From the Past

Finisher had been home for eight months. He was laying low since he'd been home from prison. He was getting his team back strong and stacking his money. He had recently brought ten new guns from his down south connect and recruited a lot of new soldiers.

A lot of guys from his block had been waiting for him to come home so they could turn G.K.B., and everybody who was getting money from his block he made them turn Blood or leave. Finisher had a lot of soldiers ready to go to war for him. He heard Mally G came home and knew he had to get revenge for his brother and best friend's death. Finisher was home laying up with his wifey.

"Baby, what's wrong with you. Why you looking like that?" she asked him.

"Nah, I'm just thinking. One of them niggas that had something to do with my lil brother getting killed just came home. I'ma finish that lil nigga when I catch him!"

"Baby, don't let no nigga stress you out. As much as you did for me. I'll kill a nigga for you myself."

"Nah baby all you gotta do is take care of our little one in your stomach. My lil problem gone be a piece of cake, I got everything planned out already. Get dressed, we about to go to the mall, though. You getting big. You need some new clothes."

★★★★★

"Jamal, you up early," India said after she opened her eyes and saw him sitting on the edge of the bed.

"My body still use to waking up early from being locked up."

"Well, its good you up early. We could go to the mall and get you some new clothes while it's still early. The clothes you got played out. I gotta get you up to date."

"Stuff like that don't even mean nothing to me no more but I'ma go cause I don't want to be tacky while I'm out with my baby. I can't embarrass you out here! Now get up and get dressed so we can get on the road."

*****

When Mally G and India pulled up at Short Hills Mall, it was just opening. They walked around the entire mall shopping. At the end of their mini-shopping spree, India had picked him out fifteen outfits. She brought herself two pairs of shoes and some lingerie. Everything they brought was purchased with a small portion of the money Shice gave him.

India carried four bags and made Mally G carried the rest. When Mally G tried to open the car door, a couple bags fell to the ground.

Finisher pulled up alongside of him right before he got the door opened.

"Oh shit! Bae, there go that nigga right there!" Finisher said before he reached under his seat and grabbed his 44 Bulldog. "I guess it was easier than I expected," Finisher said while pointing his gun at Mally G through his tinted window while rolling it down with his other hand. Pow! Pow!

*****

Over in Philly:

ZaZa's family and friends were having a get together to celebrate her birthday. Her cousins Hammer and Ditty Bop were talking to Jazmine about what happened the day she was murdered.

"So you telling me somebody was trying to off this Mally G dude, and Zakia got hit in the cross fire?" Hammer asked.

"Yeah, I saw the whole thing. She was running up trying to give him a hug when she got shot!"

"He gotta go then! My lil cousin dead because his bitch ass, and he had the audacity to not even come to her funeral! Plus, we can find out who killed ZaZa while we torturing his ass!" Hammer said.

"One time I was with Tammy, and we seen the nigga. We was at the gas station so I couldn't do what I wanted to do. Plus,

Tammy started bitching when I started shooting out her car, so the nigga got away," Ditty Bop explained.

"Why you ain't been tell me so we could kill that fool?" Hammer asked.

"I was asking Tammy where he be at, but she kept telling me she think he got locked up."

"I could find out where he be, matter of fact I could find out where he live. Tammy told me she dropped ZaZa off at his house before. I heard he got money too. As long as ya'll break me off with a lil something we could make something happen," Jazmine said.

"That ain't about nothing, if we come off you know I'ma hit you. Get that address for me," Ditty Bop said.

"Aight, I'm about to call Tammy now," Jazmine said as she pulled out her phone.

*****

Back at the mall:

Mally G reached for his bags he dropped seconds before Finisher shot, the bullets just missed his head as he bent down. India was standing on the opposite side of the car. She fell to the ground after a bullet hit her. Mally G got low and crawled around to the other side as Finisher pulled off.

"Baby, you alright?" Mally G asked terrified. All he could think about was losing India the same way he lost ZaZa. He couldn't believe this was happening again.

"I don't know. It feel like I got hit in the arm," India said before she got up and placed her hand over her right shoulder. Once air entered her open wound the pain increased dramatically. She began to groan as she reached for her shoulder. "Please, don't let me die. It hurt so bad!" she cried.

"You gone be okay, baby. Come on, I gotta get you to the hospital."

India was cryin the entire ride to the hospital. Mally G ran red lights and did whatever he had to do to get her to the hospital as soon as possible. Once they got there, India made a big scene as if she was dying. The doctors took her in immediately and checked her wound. She finally calmed down after the doctor told her that she was lucky that the bullet only pierced her skin. They cleaned her wound, patched her up, and gave her Tylenol for the pain. Mally G was relieved to know she was okay.

Two police officers entered the room just as they were about to leave. "Excuse me ma'am, but we will like to ask you some questions about how you got shot." One of the cops stopped and looked at Mally G before asking, "Were you there when the incident occurred?"

"No, he was on his way to get me from the mall when it happened," India said before Mally G got a chance to utter a single word. She wanted him out of trouble and knew if parole found out he was around a shooting it wouldn't look good.

The police took India to an empty room and asked her how she got shot. She described Finisher and his car to them and said he pulled up and started shooting at a stranger next to her and that she got hit in the crossfire. They asked a few more questions and wrote down details before they let her go.

Once they left the hospital, Mally G drove straight home. As soon as they walked in the house he said, "I'll be back. Get some rest, okay."

"No! Jamal, please don't do nothing stupid. I'm okay, I swear, baby, I don't want to lose you again," India said in between cries.

"Baby, I promise I'm coming right back, I'm not gone do nothing stupid."

"Then where you going? It ain't worth it, I'm okay!"

"I'm coming right back. Don't worry."

"What you think gone happen if you kill that guy! You're going back to jail!"

"India, I'm not going to kill nobody. I'm coming right back. I'm just going to clear my mind."

"You can clear your mind here! I promise I'll give you time to think. I won't bother you."

"India, I'm coming right back. Go lay down."

Mally G left while she sat there crying in sorrow. He pulled off and headed straight towards High Street. India started blowing his phone up as soon as he pulled off, so he cut it off. He needed time to gather his thoughts and figure out his next move.

He drove through High Street and continued until it turned into Astor Street. While driving down Astor Street he saw a crackhead he used to always serve before he started selling wholesale. She was walking up the street with her butt exposed obviously trying to catch a date. He beeped the horn twice and signaled for her to come.

"Baby, when you come home? The hood miss you, these motherfuckers been selling some garbage since you left."

"Get in real fast."

She got into his car, and then he pulled off.

"I'm surprised a fine fella like you ain't got a flock of girls to choose from now that you're home. You want some head or some coochie?"

"I don't wont neither. I just want to talk. I know you a tell me the truth, and I got some stuff to get off my chest."

Mally G desperately needed somebody to vent to, and he felt a prostitute/drug addict was the best person to talk to. She'd sell her body for drugs, she was probably homeless, and her life was messed up more than his, so she had no reason to lie to him. He started breaking down his entire life to her without mentioning names or places. He explained how he wants to leave the game alone so bad, but the life keeps pulling him back in.

He shed a tear after telling her how he felt about killing Snub. He had dreams when he was locked up about Snub asking for his life back. He knew he could have let Snub go down south, and nobody wouldn't have cared.Menace told Mally G he would've forgiven Snub, he felt he had to forgive everybody in order for God to forgive him. That added more pain to his heart knowing the person who was the victim forgave him, but he never gave Snub a chance to be forgiven.

He told her about how killing Str8 Lace caused so many people to die including his close friends Mar Mar and ZaZa. He told her about the conflict he had with his best friend Jay. The more Mally G spoke the more tears fell down his face. She told him she believed he could change, but he had to move far away so his past wouldn't catch up with him. He realized she was right; the only way he could change and live positively would be if he moved far away, if he changed his environment.

He gave her fifty dollars and dropped her back off on Astor Street, then headed home. When he pulled into his driveway, India met him at the door. She ran to him and jumped in his arms as soon as he exited the car.

"Baby, I'm so glad you're back. I was so worried," she said as tears fell down her face.

"Baby, we gotta move out of New Jersey. I went and cleared my mind and that's what I came up with."

"Whatever you want to do, I'm with you. I'll move with you to Alaska before I lose you again. I love you so much, Jamal!"

Back at Finisher's house:

"Baby, I know the guy you was shooting at," Finisher's soon-to-be babymother said.

"Where you know him from?"

"I grew up with him. Him and my brother been best friends since they were babies. He the reason my brother got shot by the cops. He told my brother some bullshit, and he got wetted up off PCP and had a shoot-out with the cops. I hate him now! My brother never forgave me to this day for what he told him."

"What he tell him?" Finisher asked curiously.

"He told him we had sex. My brother called me all types of names. Me and him never been close since. I want you to finish him too, baby. I know where his mother live. He got money too. He came up off some drugs I gave him when my brother got locked up the first time," Karen said.

Finisher was furious. the thought of Mally G having sex with Karen drove him insane. He knew he really had to get rid of Mally G, and fast.

* * * * *

Three days later:

Mally G woke up because his cell phone kept ringing.

"Baby, can you hand me my phone?"

After India handed him his phone, he noticed he had twelve missed calls from his mother. He called her back immediately to make sure everything was okay.

"Ma, what's wrong? Is everything good?" He asked when his mother answered the phone crying.

"They got my baby!" She sobbed.

"Ma, what you talking about?"

"They kidnapped Amod!"

"What? Who?"

"I don't know. They left a note saying they gone kill him. They holding him for ransom. They want you to deliver a hundred thousand dollars at 10 o'clock. Please, get my baby back! Please, Jamal!" She cried.

"Ma, I'm on my way to the house now." He hung up his phone and started getting dressed.

"Jamal, what happened?" India asked, concerned.

He took a deep breath before saying, "Somebody kidnapped Amod."

"Oh my God. What you gone do?"

"India, I really don't know. I gotta go to my mother's house, they left a note. They want ransom money delivered by me."

"Please don't go!" India said as she began to cry as she thought about losing him.

"I have to. I got him in this mess."

"Just call the police and let them handle it, baby. I don't want anything to happen to you. Please!"

"India, everything gone be alright. If I call the police, he will wind up dead for sure. I'll be back baby, don't worry."

"Jamal, do you hear yourself! How in the hell you expect me not to worry? If you going, I'm coming with you then!"

"No, I'll be back. I don't want you involved in this mess."

"I'm already involved! I'm involved with you! I'm going!" India yelled as tears ran down her face.

"Baby, I promise I'm coming back."

Mally G started heading for the door, but India blocked him. She pushed him back and said, "Jamal if you leave me again, it's over between us! Think about everything we spoke about when you was in jail. Please, don't do this to me!" She dropped to the floor and curled up as a stream of tears ran down her face.

"I'm sorry. I have to go."

Mally G left once again, leaving India at the door crying. He called Shice as soon as he got into his car. He explained everything that was going on.

"So what you wanna do, bruh?" Shice asked.

"I don't know, but I gotta do something."

"Who you think is behind this?"

"I'm almost 100% sure this is Finisher's work."

"Aight, I'ma meet you at your mother house," Shice said before hanging up.

Mally G mind was doing a million miles per hour as he drove to his mother's house. *Damn, why the fuck I ain't been move my mother out the hood. It's all my fault this dumb shit happened! I can't believe this nigga a take it this far. He shot my girl, now this. I swear if he kill my brother, I'ma kill everybody he love and know. Damn, why am I'm thinking like this? Everything gone be okay. I hope everything be okay! Damn, my mother will never forgive me if they kill Amod. I hope they don't kill my lil brother. What the fuck! How the hell I'ma get out of this shit.*

When he pulled up to his mother's house, she ran out of the house crying.

"Please, get my baby back! Please!"

"Ma calm down, I need to be focused. Where the letter at! Where the letter at, ma?"

She finally calmed down after he took her into his arms. She sobbed a few words into his chest that he couldn't understand, then stepped back and handed him the letter.

His heart was bumping one hundred miles per hour as he read on*:*

> ***This letter is for Mally G. If you ever want to see ya lil brother alive again, get a hundred thousand dollars ready. A-Wall said he left his cell phone in his top draw in his room. I'ma call at 10 o'clock tonight. Only you can deliver the money. See you at ten. And remember calling the cops is like signing a death certificate! From your worst nightmare.***

Mally G went into A-Wall's room to get the phone. He opened the draw and there it was: his cell phone next to a bulletproof vest and two P89 17 shot Rugers. He picked up one of the handguns and stared at it as it sat in his hands.

To be continued…

Words from the author

My name is Naeem Kearney, but I'm known in the streets as Na Blood. I was born and raised in Newark, NJ. I attended and graduated 99-03 from Malcolm X Shabazz High School. I joined a gang at the young age of fifteen and worked my way up in ranks as a Sex Money Murda member. Most of my life, I was in and out of jail. I spent a majority of my 20's in prison. I wrote this book in 2009, during the last 6 months of my bid and wrote part 2 since my release.

I was mostly known for my music. Me and my little brother King Braize released a mixtape *Welcome to Murdaville* in 2005, which took the streets by storm. A lot of people at the time had our ringtones on their phones when chirp phones was in high demand. Writing is something I just tried, and it worked out for me because I was always good at expressing myself but music was my first passion. However, I fell in love with writing and will choose it over music, and I put my heart into my work.

Now I'm retired from the streets and gang lifestyle and am fully focused on building my career as an entrepreneur. Basically, I still have my same hustler's mentality, but the difference now is everything I do is legitimate. I own my own publishing company REALRIGHT PUBLISHING, but this is only the beginning of my journey. I plan on being the owner of multiple businesses and eventually becoming a millionaire.

I'm currently working as a CDL licensed truck driver. Me and my little brother Aquil Williams, also known as King Braize, own a record label, Korruption Records that's under our main branch KROWN movement. We also have an embroidery line called Krownwear. Check out King Braize app, it's in all app stores on your electronic devices.

I'm a four-time convicted felon and have been to prison three different times. I graduated high school in 2003 and didn't learn anything because learning wasn't my main focus. I can admit I learned more in jail then I learned in school, only because I made learning my priority. Now that I'm not in jail, I go to bookstores and still read to further my knowledge.

Anything you wanna be or do you can learn if you put your mind to it. After I wrote this book I came home and tried to use the streets as a steppingstone to build my company. I ended up doing a county bid, then a prison bid in New York, wasting more valuable time out of my life. This time I got a job and tried the legitimate way and things have never been so good in my life. I don't worry about police, stick up boys, beef, or no drama. I'm highly respected in my hood still, but I live for me now!

My message to the youth and anybody that feel like you're trapped in the streets is, "IF I CAN DO IT, YOU CAN!" You just have to really want something different out of life and have to take the steps to make things different. Just keep in mind, sometimes you have to be different to make a difference, and if you don't change nothing will!

Aknowledgements

First of all, I would like to thank myself for putting the effort in and believing that I can do it. I will like to thank all the people that supported my music and book.

The streets made me who I am, so I want to thank everyone that crossed paths with me throughout my struggle. This was kind of easy for me being as though I have experienced so much throughout my journey in the street life.

I will like to thank my mother Regina Bryant Kearney for bringing me into this world and being the best mother ever. Also, for pushing me to do the right thing and staying by my side when I was right or wrong. I told you I was going to leave the streets alone and do something positive and look now, I'm an author! :)

I would like to thank my aunts Shahida Garrett, Sherry Garrett, and Waynatte Counts for being there throughout my whole life like three more mothers.

Shahida aka Syeda, you was like a sister and aunt. Thanks for believing in me and holding me up when I was down. Na Na Love you!

Sherry you were like my mother foreal! Thanks for taking care of us when my mother wasn't there because of work, and I miss your cooking too.

Waynatte aka Aunt Dot, you was the backbone to our family as far back as I can remember, so thanks for everything. Words can't express how thankful I am for having you in my life.

I will like to thank my father for helping bring me into this world. I know you weren't there for me as I was growing up, and I forgive you. No love lost, my nigga!

I will like to thank all my brothers and sisters, Exzabia aka Unique, Malik aka Muk, Peter aka Pete, Sonya, Samone, Derrand aka Hammer, Amber aka Auntie!, Emil aka Ditty Bop, Amirrah, Virgil aka Brazy Boy, India, Ramel aka Jigga man a hundred grand, Jada, and all the possibles my father have...lol

Shot out to my other mothers: Rochelle Kelly and Keisha Williams. Thanks for holding me down and pushing me to stay focused!

Love you grandma!!! R.I.P. Odessa Kearney. Love you grandpa!!! R.I.P. Richard Johnson.

I will like to thank Breeze for typing my book out.

My favorite 3 cousins Jarod aka Spaz! Whats Grappin Cuzzo lol. Bang aka Snook you more on the brother side so you already know! And Aggy Kia lol. Love you to the moon and back! Thanks for the proofreading and finding the mistakes I missed!

My boy Blimp wat's the deal! You taught me a lot of shit in these street. Hold ya head bruh, you a real nigga!

My boys SM, what's good bruh! You a real nigga! You already know we brothers for life it ain't too much to say!

My best friend Ayesha "Esh" Collins, I love you, bestie! I'm sad you moved so far but I'm happy for you. I miss you like crazy!

Shot out to my brother from another Menace, wat's good pimping! You know the shit!

My boy Sunny Kapone wat's good. Stay focused on ya music, you better than you think!

My boy Davy, thanks for helping me get my life together. You already know we brothers for life!

Antwan aka Big Baby I hope you still in there getting ya books right. Can't wait until you come home too. Stop wilding in there and make it home. Da hood missing you, bruh.

My nigga Skoot wats good. You already know the shit!

My Ex Kia what's good my nigga. We done been through it all and our friendship is still unbreakable.

Can't Forget my BroGods Spirit and Brother Sammad! Ya'll already know it's only up from here on!

Free ALL my niggaz that's doing time. Don't let the time do you! Take advantage and learn something that can help you in the future. Free my brothers Ditty & Jigg! Free my nigga Zak, Greez & Bandanna!

Shot out to my circle on the "A" Love ya'll!

Oddey and Tamara Blanding thanks for staying on my ass and telling me to do the right thing, I really appreciate it.

Shot out all my niggas I lost to the struggle... **R.I.P** Bem, LB, Odey O, DJ, Gary, Bo, Bee, Bleek, Ern, Kanye, T-Turn, House, Su, Weezy, Bishop, Copo, Roc, Naim, Billy, Melvin, Shock (ITB), T-Man, Copo 7, Randsom, Shane, Purto Roc, Rocky, Uncle Bubble, Hass (brick towers) and anybody else that died in the struggle.

All my other niggas that didn't get personal shoutouts don't feel no type of way! Love yall too… maybe lol

I'm not gone name names cuz shit crazy in da hood but all my real niggas know who ya'll are! Love dat nigga!

Make sure ya'll check out the soundtrack to this book. It's fire!!!! www.realrightpublishing.com

Contact info:

If you're serious about your work and looking to get your work published contact me at:

Website: www.realrightpublishing.com
Facebook: Naeem Kearney
Instagram: Nablazer
Emails: realrightpubishing@gmail.com
nablazermusic@gmail.com

RealRightPublishing accepts manuscripts from jail as well!

No money down!
Get your work Published today!

AVAILABLE AT: RealRightPublishing.com
Follow me at
IG: Nablazer
FB: Naeem Kearney

Made in the USA
Middletown, DE
03 March 2023

26132716R00116